STRANGERS IN THE NIGHT

A NOVEL

RAYMOND S FLEX

The night air played tricks with the eyes.

And the darkness layered in over everything.

In the near distance, he could hear the sound of the string quartet. Its harmonies, though, standing here on the marble balcony, came and went in waves. Just tiny, little snatches of song.

Nothing at all to dig an ear into.

He clung to his chilly flute of champagne, still feeling the bitter tingle of the bubbles on his tongue from his most recent taste. He could smell the rose garden down below, unseen, but still there, and, further off, he could hear the hum of the motorway.

Quite a lot of traffic tonight.

On New Year's Eve.

He leaned over the wall of the balcony, making sure there was no bird excrement before he propped up his tuxedoed elbow on the marble.

He stared out into the darkness of the garden; glad, in a

way, that unlike all the other large country homes he had visited for some party or other there were none of those floodlights.

No floodlights to render the trellises, the carefully pruned gravelled garden paths, the iced-over ponds, as some never-ending, nightmare museum piece.

He could feel her.

Standing in the opening of the French doors.

Behind him.

If he was only to turn around, he would see her.

And she would see him.

PART 1
TWO DANCERS

THE INSISTENT RAIN

Mitts *could hear* the rain water dripping down his bedroom's ventilation hatch. He heard it drum into the stainless-steel guttering system, collect for maybe a minute or so, and then slide, in one single pool, all the way along and down to the dirt ground outside.

With a distant, but profound, metal-intoned *splash*.

It wasn't the rain that had woken him.

It was something else.

At the back of his throat, Mitts could still taste the processed tomatoes from the sauce his father had served for dinner that evening. When he breathed in, he caught the scent of the sauce still clinging to his skin. And it melded with the smell of the rain.

The smell of something else.

It sent a slight chill through him.

Mitts tugged his ragged, wool blanket up over his thin, bare chest, and shuddered long and hard, hoping that the cold sensation would pass.

What time was it?

Mitts's bedroom was dark, and foreboding. But it never got any better.

Not with the morning light. Not in tomorrow's sunshine.

Not *ever*.

The Compound would never be his home.

But Mitts understood that feeling at home wasn't the point.

This was about survival.

Nothing else mattered now.

His parents had only allowed him to open the ventilation hatch a couple of days ago. That decision had been based on Doctor Heinmein's advice.

Heinmein had come to skulk about Mitts's bedroom, in the middle of the afternoon, about a week ago. He had arrived with a device which emitted otherworldly sounding interference:

Electronic *squeals*.

Bip-bip-bips.

And what sounded to Mitts like computerised *groans*.

Just like it had been all along, Mitts's parents assumed that he knew nothing about what was going on. They figured him as just some dumb kid: because, at eleven years old, what could Mitts *really* know about what was going on?

4

But, just like everyone else, he had seen the news reports.

He'd experienced the *frenzy*.

The *panic* that night when . . . when he'd been forced to . . . it was better not to think about it for now.

It would only start him off crying again.

As Mitts propped himself up on his elbow, the springs of his camp bed made a series of dampened *shrieks*. He reached out for his wristwatch which lay on the upturned plastic case beside his bed. The glow-in-the-dark display told him that it'd just gone five in the morning.

He wrapped the watch about his wrist.

When he sniffed, he placed the smell in the air as disinfectant:

Coming from outside.

Through the ventilation hatch.

Whenever Mitts smelled *that* smell he always thought of radiation. Of the stuff which had brought the world crumbling down.

Brought the world, for all intents and purposes, to a slow and steady halt.

Mitts shrugged off his blanket and stepped down onto the bare, ice-cold laminate flooring.

Back home, back in his *real* bedroom, Mitts had had a thick carpet. He hadn't appreciated it until he had arrived here, to the Compound, to his new 'home'. But he knew now that having a carpet spread beneath the bare soles of his feet was a privilege.

Like always, Mitts had on only a pair of pyjama bottoms: the ones with the green-and-gold tartan design; the ones which were well-worn, and which his mother, about a week before they left home, had talked about having thrown out so that he might get a new pair.

Nobody talked about throwing things out now.

Not anymore.

Mitts mashed the light switch beside his bed with his fist, and the too-bright, fluorescent strip lighting blinked into life. It shone its steady glow over the whole of Mitts's bedroom.

Mitts yawned and then padded over to the ventilation hatch, the smell of disinfectant coming stronger still now. One thing that Mitts loathed above all else about his 'bed-room' was how tall the ceiling was. He had never thought about the low-down ceiling in his bedroom back home making it seem more cosy, but that was definitely the case.

The ventilation hatch was high up on the wall, and Mitts had been told, in no uncertain terms, by both parents, on separate occasions, that he wasn't to mess with it.

Could they *really* blame his curiosity?

As Mitts had planned it long ago, in one of those fits of boredom that was par for the course about the Compound, he headed over to the large, plastic container in the corner.

The one which was stuffed full of his possessions.

All he had been able to collect together before he had fled his home with his mother and father.

Mitts slid the plastic container along the floor, making a

teeth-grating scraping noise that he hoped wouldn't wake his parents, or Heinmein.

When he brought it just beneath the ventilation hatch, he clambered up on top of the plastic container, feeling it support his weight without too much difficulty.

People—other kids, teachers—had always described Mitts as 'wiry', 'spry', or, in low voices that they *believed* he couldn't hear, 'a streak of piss'.

That last description wasn't helped by his blindingly blond hair.

As Mitts stood on the plastic container, the smell of disinfectant became nothing less than a stench. It bit at Mitts's nostrils. Sent a swirling, *dizzying* sensation right down to his gut. He tasted the tomato sauce at the back of his throat. Stopped for a moment, forced himself to keep it down. He could still hear the rain dripping down the other end of the ventilation hatch.

Drip. Drip. Drip.

Steadier now.

Less frequent.

Soon it would stop raining completely.

Mitts couldn't so much as turn his nose in the general direction of the ventilation hatch without feeling overpowered by the stench of disinfectant.

Whatever it was . . . whatever was causing that stink . . . it was *up there*, sitting right by the exterior hatch.

Mitts peered through the metal slats of the ventilation

hatch. He had often fantasised about peeling off the hatch and crawling through it. As he lay on his side, on his camp bed back down in the middle of the room, he would wonder to himself if he might be able to fit through it.

Why, it would be a whole other world inside.

He looked to the hatch, saw that it was held in place by four sturdy screws—one in each corner.

He didn't have tools to take care of that.

Not here.

Mitts continued to peer through the slats for another few moments, and then he felt his chest tighten again. What was it? Something had changed. It took him a moment to realise it. The smell, the *stink* of disinfectant. It had lessened now. Mitts could hardly smell it, let alone feel the burn passing through his airways.

Mitts had to strain himself to so much as *sniff* out a remainder.

Whatever it was . . . whatever had been hanging about at his hatch . . . it was gone now.

———

At breakfast, as always, as per his parents' instructions, Mitts was fully dressed.

This morning he wore a white V-necked t-shirt, grey-blue jeans, and a pair of battered trainers that he'd used for PE back when he'd had to go to school.

Back when 'school' had existed.

He didn't have to do PE now.

Thank *God*.

The kitchen was farcically large—Mitts often thought about that word he'd learned in his last week of English: 'farcical', it seemed so apt for right now.

The kitchen was all stainless steel. Enormous, blocky counters, all shining in the bright, even light. The sinks were like bathtubs. And the central, steel surface, which they made their kitchen table, was easily large enough to seat thirty. They all needed high stools to sit comfortably, or else they had to precariously balance a chair atop a pile of books, or a sturdy box sourced from somewhere or other in the Compound.

'All' of them was Mitts, his mother, his father, and Heinmein.

His father stood over one of the more modest stoves, cooking up scrambled eggs from a powdered mixture. Just like always, he wore a shirt.

For some reason, when Mitts had left home—when they had come *here*—Mitts had believed that his whole family would be reduced to sitting about all day in tracksuits. All of them in comfort clothing. But, no, it was quite an insistent feature of the Compound. His father demanded that Mitts— his father demanded that he himself—wear normal, daytime clothes.

Items which, as his father might put it, 'they'd be happy

leaving the house in'.

The shirt that Mitts's father specifically wore that day was a chequered design, with a base of sailcloth white, with bridging purple lines over the top. He cooked with his shirt sleeves rolled up and with several of the buttons down the front undone . . . it could get pretty hot at the stove, with all the metal around.

Underneath, his father wore a pair of smart, black jeans, loafers on his feet.

One thing was for certain, his father would be prepared to meet and greet just about anybody who might stop by at the Compound.

A real shame that the rest of the world was dead.

Whenever Mitts sat in the kitchen, he couldn't help but breathe in the bloody smell of metal all about him. He knew that he would never get used to *that* smell. The smell which reminded him of all those times—those *countless* times—when he had gone and cut himself somehow.

But, as his father went about serving out the eggs for Mitts and himself, knocking off the excess with a pair of *clangs* of the metal serving spoon against the side of the pan, Mitts couldn't help catching a pre-taste of that delicious, buttery mixture in his mouth.

Mitts hadn't been able to sleep since that stench of disinfectant had woken him, and so he'd really built up a ravenous hunger.

Every time he moved on his stool, it seemed, his stomach groaned in protest.

Back on the stove, Mitts watched the steam curl up from the metal jug of coffee.

Although he loved the smell of coffee, he couldn't stand the taste.

Once, during his first days here, at the Compound, when everything had been so different, it had seemed like a time for trying new things. And when his father had offered him some coffee, he had accepted.

But it'd tasted like ash in his mouth.

His father sat down beside him at the enormous, stainless-steel table.

He immediately tucked into his eggs with obvious appetite.

Mitts studied his father for a few moments before turning his attention onto his own breakfast. As he forked his way through his eggs, as he popped each mouthful in through his lips, he thought about how the Compound had changed everything.

How, back when they'd lived at home, it'd been his mother who'd always cooked breakfast.

She'd always been the one who cleaned up after them, too.

Now, though, those roles had become reversed.

It was a rarity to see his mother out of bed before midday.

And still with dark circles clinging to her eye sockets.

Mitts had got about halfway through his scrambled eggs, and they were really helping to send his hunger packing, when he heard the uneven gait of Heinmein.

Plod.

Sweep.

Plod.

Sweep.

The way that Heinmein walked reminded Mitts of Igor, at least the Igor from the cartoons he'd seen; Doctor Frankenstein's assistant. How Igor would drag his crippled leg behind him.

Although there were plenty of crutches, and other mobility apparatus, scattered through the Compound, Heinmein didn't seem bothered with using a single one of them.

At first, Mitts had thought that it might be pride which prevented Heinmein from using something to help him walk upright, but, in the end, he decided that it was all about obsession.

Namely that Heinmein was so deep down in those experiments he spent his days and *nights* on that he was rendered absentminded to pretty much all mundane, routine tasks:

Feeding himself.

Washing.

Walking upright.

Mitts eyed Heinmein as he *plod-swept* his way into the kitchen.

With a muttered greeting to Mitts and his father, Heinmein approached the large saucepan filled with scrambled eggs.

Mitts felt a slight tightening sensation in his chest. Although he knew he should be thankful, that Heinmein had been the one to warn them of the impending disaster, that he had been the one to bring them *here* when all others were evacuating the Compound, he couldn't quite extend that gratitude to *liking* the man.

Perhaps it was his unkempt, too-long, greying black hair that stuck up in tufts, looking as if Heinmein had a bush sprouting from his scalp.

Or maybe it was how he constantly wore the same tattered lab coat—*day and night*—with some withered shirt underneath, all covered with holes, unironed.

His left shoe had a large hole where his sweaty, socked toes peeped through.

He was—at least to Mitts's mind—pretty much the stereotype of the mad professor.

Even just having his father be in the same room as Heinmein, to see his father's towering two-metre-high stature against the doctor's diminutive just-about one-sixty-five, seemed a touch unfair.

Whenever Heinmein wanted to look Mitts's father in the eye, he had to tilt his head back and squint slightly through his thick-framed—well-dented, well-*cracked*—glasses.

After having scooped a helping of scrambled eggs onto one of the metal plates, and sticking a fork into them for good measure, Heinmein *plod-swept* his way back out of the kitchen, leaving Mitts and his father alone.

Like always, Mitts had finished up his breakfast first. And so he watched his father chewing away, patiently, on his scrambled eggs, a cup of coffee smoking away before him.

Mitts breathed in those strong waves and found them a little dizzying.

"Dad?" Mitts said.

"Mm," his father replied, in such a way that, Mitts was sure, had their roles been reversed, his father would've scolded him for having his mouth full.

"Last night, did you, I dunno, smell anything . . . anything *weird?*"

His father reached out and took a swig of his coffee. As he replaced the cup on the steel surface, he swallowed down his mouthful and then said, "What'd you mean?"

"Well, there was this . . . strange smell coming through my ventilation hatch."

"Did you tell Doctor Heinmein?"

Mitts felt his blood run hot as he anticipated the scolding.

There was no need for Mitts to reply to his father's question.

His father knew him well enough to interpret the answer.

"Mitts," his father said, with a slight sigh, "you know the procedure, any changes in environment—any change to the temperature, any odd smells, anything like that, and you're to go to Doctor Heinmein."

Mitts's father hoiked himself up off his stool. He grasped for Mitts's empty plate—not so much as a *scrap* of scrambled egg still stuck to it—and, stacking it on top of his own, headed back over to the kitchen area where he deposited both in the sink with a loud *clunk.*

He glanced back over his shoulder at Mitts.

His expression was sober.

"Come on," he said, "let's go tell him, okay?"

Although Mitts would rather have stayed sat on his stool in the kitchen all day—with all the boredom that particular decision might entail—he resigned himself to doing his duty.

What had to be done.

In the name of survival.

———

"Doctor?" Mitts's father said, rapping his knuckles against the partially opened door.

The scurrying sound of human knuckles against the metal door sent a quiver through Mitts's stomach. He would never get used to *that* sound either.

Although Mitts tried his best to limit his interactions with Heinmein to a bare minimum, he always noticed, when he reluctantly had to come to Doctor Heinmein's office for whatever reason, that the air smelled of stale oranges and cheesy feet.

It brought the scrambled eggs up to the back of his throat

in the same way that smelling the disinfectant wafting through his ventilation hatch early that morning had brought along a reminder of that tomato sauce his father had cooked the night before.

Heinmein had his back to them. As always, his office was a cluttered mess. He had papers piled up all around him. His head blocked the radiation-white light of the CRT computer screen before him:

A model from the *last* century.

Beside Heinmein, at his elbow, Mitts observed the emptied plate of scrambled eggs.

There was no sign of cutlery.

Mitts wondered if Heinmein had used any at all.

Mitts casually slipped a glance up to the door, saw the name engraved on the metal tag there:

DR H HEINMEIN.

It was something of a wonder to Mitts that, in all of the Compound, Heinmein remained in what had previously been his office.

For one, Heinmein's office was absolutely tiny. There were *tonnes* of rooms which would've made better offices than Heinmein's. It wasn't anything more than a broom cupboard, really.

When Mitts glanced down to the laminate flooring, he saw that there was a thin mattress all bundled up into the corner of the room. There was no blanket. Nothing else. And

Mitts supposed that Heinmein simply slept in the clothes he wore during the day.

That would explain an awful lot, thinking about it . . .

"Mm?" Heinmein said, not turning around, or shifting his attention away from the computer screen.

Mitts's father looked to him, arching an eyebrow.

No matter how much Mitts wanted to get away from Heinmein—and his *office*—he took a deep breath and blurted it out.

"This morning," Mitts said, "I smelled this, I dunno, *disinfectant*-like smell wafting in through my ventilation hatch."

Heinmein didn't respond.

As was completely normal.

On other occasions, when Mitts had been forced into some sort of interaction with him, Heinmein hadn't responded until several hours later, resuming the conversation as if they'd spoken only seconds before.

Heinmein tapped away at his computer keyboard, just a whole bunch of clicking of spring-loaded plastic.

Mitts wondered if he should repeat himself, but he knew, even from the few weeks they'd been living in the Compound, that it was really not worthwhile.

He would get no reply from Heinmein.

As if to tell his father 'I told you so', Mitts turned back to him and gave him an eye-roll, coupled with a shrug of his shoulders.

Mitts's father gave him a scolding glare then turned to face Heinmein himself. Or, at least, to face the back of Heinmein's head.

"Doctor, did you hear? There might be some sort of a malfunction in the cooling system."

Heinmein tapped out something rapid-fire on his computer keyboard. Then he stopped.

Still with his back to them, he tilted his head to one side, as if one of the many papers which littered his desk had caught his attention.

Mitts took the opportunity to examine Heinmein's computer screen. But it was somewhat disappointing. He had somehow built up, in his mind, that despite all of Heinmein's personal-hygiene failings, he would be working on something so stunning—so absolutely *brilliant*—that his detachment from reality would all be understandable.

But all Mitts saw on the screen was a series of charts: coloured statistics, the kind which he might get asked to produce in his second or third year of *primary* school.

That was the thing about older people, they seemed so out-of-kilter with technology.

So unable to help themselves.

Mitts had gone about the Compound some days, through all the areas he was permitted to travel through. In almost every one of the dozens of rooms there were many computers.

Whenever he tried to fire them up, though, whenever he jabbed the power switch on their monitors, they were totally dead. And they had seemed like *far* newer systems than the one which Heinmein was currently using.

Mitts supposed that Heinmein had done something to disable them.

Oh, Mitts knew that, even if the internet still existed, there was no one left out there to communicate with, but, still, he couldn't help wanting to put his hands back on a touchscreen . . . a *keyboard* if he really had to make do.

It was strange to think, before he and his family had arrived to the Compound, he had hardly gone a day without laying his hands on some form of computer.

For the longest time, Mitts was certain Heinmein—his head still tilted to one side; his back to them—would respond to what he had said, that he would relieve the pressure which'd built up in the little, broom-cupboard office.

But, no . . .

Without any sort of acknowledgement that he had heard either Mitts or his father, Heinmein resumed his typing on that ancient computer. When Mitts listened in carefully, he could hear Heinmein muttering something to himself, under his breath.

Mitts felt his father squeeze his shoulder.

And, with a knowing glance, his father steered him away from Heinmein's office.

Mitts could *breathe* again . . .

———

Mitts pressed his ear up against the cool metal door of his bedroom.

He listened for footsteps.

For the faintest sound of breathing.

Could hear nothing.

But it was best to be sure.

Soon after he and his father had returned from Heinmein's office, his father had gone off to wash up in the kitchen. It was then that Mitts had ventured into one of the unfrequently visited maintenance cupboards which was located right at the very edge of the Restricted Area:

The area within the Compound where Mitts and his family—Doctor Heinmein—all lived.

At the end of the corridor, Mitts had been confronted with the sign on the inside of the blast door. The no-nonsense, high-vis, red-and-yellow stripes behind it.

RESTRICTED AREA

And then, a little below, a notice in white lettering with a black background which read:

For emergency lock-release, push button.

Apparently having been briefed by Heinmein, the very first thing Mitts's mother and father had sworn him against doing was pressing that button.

Like a naughty toddler, Mitts had felt that tingle down in the base of his gut.

His eyes had traced the wall, the red button, covered by a

breakable, glass box, and he had wondered what would happen if he *did* punch it.

Would a toxic, sulphur-smelling, smog billow in through the opening?

Suffocating them all?

Killing them all?

Mitts recalled when they'd been back home, when his parents had made a similar threat to him.

That time, though, they had implored him *not* to put his hand down the hole in the kitchen sink, that, because of the garbage-disposal blades nestled within, he could do himself terrible harm.

But that had been different.

Then Mitts would've lost a few fingers.

If he pressed that button now he would—in all likelihood —bring an end to humanity.

Mitts brought his ear away from his bedroom door. His ear ached a little, and he realised that he'd been pressing it a little too hard against the metal. That was the thing about the Compound, everything was built so that it might perform some no-frills purpose.

Back home, if he'd pressed his ear up against his bedroom door, all he would've experienced was the slightly warm wood.

Just thinking about *wood* now sent his nostrils tingling.

He could almost smell it . . . and, yet, he felt like he had forgotten what it smelled like at all.

Just as he had forgotten what fresh fruit tasted like, or how the sun felt against his skin.

Satisfied that nobody was coming, Mitts trod away from his bedroom door, and, as he had done earlier that morning, he brought the large plastic container which contained his possessions over so that it rested just below the maintenance hatch.

From the waistband of his jeans, Mitts removed the half dozen screwdrivers he had concealed.

All the screwdrivers had the same gunmetal-coloured, plastic handle, but they were all of varying sizes.

He hadn't been one-hundred-percent certain which one he needed.

As Mitts had returned from the maintenance cupboard, he had been paranoid that his father would pop up from somewhere. That, at first, he would smile at Mitts.

But then he imagined his father turning his attention onto his waistband, asking what he had concealed there. And then Mitts would have to explain.

Thankfully, though, he had got back to his bedroom without bumping into anyone.

Mitts laid the screwdrivers on his camp bed, and then glanced up at the maintenance hatch, judging the screws by sight alone. He grabbed hold of one of the screwdrivers, leaped up on the plastic container, tried it out.

Nope.

He tossed that one back onto the bed.

Tried another.

Nope.

Another.

Nothing.

Mitts glanced down at the remaining screwdrivers. He plucked up one which seemed to be *far* too small. But he gave it a go, anyway.

He felt the screwdriver slip into the head.

He turned.

The screwdriver *gripped*.

But it didn't move.

Mitts sunk his teeth into his lower lip. He put all the force he could muster into turning the screw. But it wouldn't budge.

Not at all.

He must've spent a good minute or so trying to turn the screwdriver. And he only stopped when he tasted blood. Felt it trickle down his chin.

With a frustrated *grunt*, Mitts tossed the screwdriver off behind him, in the direction of the camp bed. But he heard it miss. He heard it clatter down onto the laminate flooring.

Sucking on his bloodied lip, Mitts barged into his en-suite bathroom, flipped on the light above the mirror, and took a look at himself.

Once he'd soaked a wad of toilet paper in cold water and was pressing it hard against his lower lip, he found himself staring back at his own reflection.

Even in the bright, even light, Mitts could tell that he looked pale.

His eyes sunken in their sockets.

Though Mitts had often heard people—usually his mother—describing his eyes as being a hazel-green colour; he thought that now they looked a little more of a *sludge*-brown.

Every week—every Sunday evening—Heinmein would give each of them: Mitts, his mother and his father; a check-up.

Heinmein would take their pulse, their blood pressure, a blood sample, and, of course, he would weigh each of them.

Although Heinmein never showed any sort of emotion as he scrawled the information down on his *prehistoric* clip-board, Mitts had noticed, each week, that he had been losing weight.

About a kilo a week average.

And though Mitts had never been the most robust of kids —he had broken more bones . . . had had more bones *broken* .. . than any other kid at school—even he thought that he had got scrawnier since they'd arrived at the Compound.

Mitts could see the way his clothing hung off his frame.

Sometimes Mitts allowed his dislike of Heinmein to over-whelm him, and he actually got around to blaming him—even if only in his own mind—for his mother's state of health.

He thought that the weekly check-ups were only really a way of making him and his family feel deeply anxious.

They'd got Mitts feeling anxious, hadn't they?

Satisfied that the bleeding had stopped, Mitts tossed the bloodied wad of paper into the toilet bowl. It landed with a *splash*.

As Mitts stepped out of his bathroom, and back into his bedroom, he promised himself that one thing was for certain. That he wasn't going to allow Heinmein to tell him and his family what to do.

Even if his father was too naïve to see it, Mitts wouldn't allow Heinmein to harm him or his family just because they *trusted* him.

———

Back up on the plastic container, Mitts continued to work at the screws.

Already, he could feel the fatigue webbing along the back of his right hand as he worked to undo the screw. And he was only about halfway to unscrewing the first of the four screws.

He supposed that these ventilation hatches had been installed using an electric screwdriver, that was how it'd got so tight. And Mitts cursed himself for being so *weedy*, for not having any of those *muscles* the sporty kids had. He knew that if one of those kids had been here, in Mitts's situation right now, they would've got these screws out in a heartbeat.

Off, over his shoulder, Mitts heard a cough.

Out in the corridor.

He stopped dead.

His heart in his mouth.

Arms raised over his head.

Screwdriver pressed hard into the screw.

He listened out, hoping whoever was there would slip off into the distance.

A pair of knocks on his door.

Clean, metallic.

Resounding.

Mitts urged himself back to his task, this time shifting his focus from *undoing* to *tightening*. His aching wrist spun the screwdriver around, working the screw back into its place. It was much easier for him to get it back where it had been now that he had loosened it.

That done, Mitts jumped down off the container, tossed the screwdriver onto his blanket on his camp bed and then bundled it up, shoved it to the foot of his mattress.

He turned to his bedroom door, wondering if, whoever was there, had heard all the commotion he had been making.

Maybe they had heard it *all*.

Knew *just* what he was up to.

Mitts slumped on his bed, breathing in deeply, trying to urge his pulse to return to somewhere near its normal rate. Finally, when Mitts supposed that he could wait no longer, he called out, a little too loudly, and with his voice cracking, "Come in!"

Without any pause, the hinges of Mitts's bedroom door squealed out.

And Heinmein appeared in the gap.

Like before—like *all* the times before—Heinmein bore the device.

Mitts took in the form of the device, its beige casing, the analogue dial with the needle currently lying propped against the Zero reading.

Heinmein hadn't switched it on yet.

Heinmein dragged his leg behind him into Mitts's room, and Mitts instantly felt a chill pass through his chest. Pass through his blood.

Heinmein mumbled something beneath his breath, but, other than that, he made no signal or sign of acknowledging that Mitts was even there at all.

In the first few days that Mitts and his family had arrived here, Mitts had been startled to discover—often in the middle of the night—Heinmein's form skulking about his room.

The sweet smell of rotten oranges, and the biting odour of cheesy feet.

How that odour had got stuck in Mitts's throat, just as it got caught in Mitts's throat right now.

That device in Heinmein's hands, purring along to itself.

The odd *squeal* and *screech* here and there.

In the darkness.

It was only when he told his father about these nightly visitations, that they came to a stop.

Mitts's father stopping Heinmein invading his bedroom at all hours of the night was one of his father's *few* interventions in Heinmein's otherwise free rein within the Compound.

As Mitts observed Heinmein going about his work now, he pulled his knees up to his chest and watched him over his kneecaps.

Just as with any other time, Heinmein remained off in his own world—seemingly occupied within his own mind. He had flipped his device on now, and he was limping about the room. Aside from the odd *screech* or *squeal*, there was hardly so much as a tiny deviation from the ordinary, background-level *clicking*.

Nothing like it had been the first few days.

Those occasions when Mitts had awoken in his bedroom to hear those *squeals* coming from the device.

And how Mitts would cling to his blanket, trying to instil some sort of warmth in his body.

Only when he had heard his bedroom door slam behind Heinmein, heard the sound of Heinmein's *plodding, sweeping* gait disappear off down the corridor did Mitts realise that it wasn't the temperature at all.

That it had been fright.

Mitts watched as Heinmein approached the ventilation hatch.

He scolded himself for not having had the presence of mind to think about moving the plastic container back to where it was normally located. He had left it right beneath the ventilation hatch.

Now, though, at least Mitts would have a clear view of his container, both because he had the lights in his bedroom turned on and because it was close by.

That was the other thing about the first few days in the Compound.

Following those night-time visitations, Mitts would always notice some of his personal possessions had gone missing from his plastic container.

He knew what it meant.

That his possessions were *unsafe* to keep.

That they might be putting their lives in danger.

But, still, Mitts found it something of a violation.

And that was why he had asked his father to put a stop to it.

Sure, the world might've ended, but that didn't mean Mitts should have to deal with a stranger skulking about in the darkness. Waking him up in the middle of the night. Rummaging through his possessions on the pretence of 'keeping them safe'.

Heinmein gripped tight to his device, making it purr as he waved it up in the air, in the direction of the ventilation hatch. He frowned to himself, screwing up his eyes behind his thick glasses. He was totally focused on the device before him.

On the dial.

Thinking that all his books were stuffed into the plastic

container at Heinmein's feet, Mitts realised he couldn't do anything other than fix his gaze on that dial.

See whether there was any movement.

See whether or not doom might be near.

Heinmein shook his head some more, muttered to himself again, and then flipped the switch on the device. Brought all those *chirps* and *chuckles* to a halt.

It was then that he turned, his black-grey hair all sticking up in tufts, and he looked straight back into Mitts's eyes.

For a long time, Mitts felt every muscle in his body draw taut.

He could do nothing but stare back into those black eyes of Heinmein's, almost losing himself in those endless pits. And then, out of nowhere, for what was the very first time Mitts could recall, Heinmein gave him a smirk.

A chill ran through him.

Heinmein turned away, headed for the door, his job, for the time being, done here.

It was only when Heinmein was halfway across the room that Mitts summoned the strength—summoned the *will* —to speak.

"The smell's gone," Mitts said.

Heinmein stopped still.

He kept his back to Mitts, the device still grasped in his hands.

The stench of rotten oranges and the sour note of cheesy feet seemed to reach its zenith.

Mitts tasted bile at the back of his throat.

It burned there.

He wished he had said nothing at all.

Why *had* he said anything?

Heinmein had been leaving him alone.

And now he was lurking there.

Because of Mitts.

Heinmein breathed in deeply, his shoulders slinking up and back.

Mitts reassured himself that Heinmein was only a smudge taller than he was. That, if it came to it, if things came down to physical blows, then Mitts could easily take him.

That was what Mitts told himself anyway.

Mitts wondered if Heinmein would *say* something to him, if he would actually act like a *human being*. But Heinmein's attention was drawn downward now.

Down to the laminate flooring at his feet.

He held still for another fraction of a second and then, in a gentle, swooping arc, he reached down. It was a physical movement which, if Mitts hadn't witnessed it himself, he would've believed Heinmein incapable of.

When Heinmein straightened back up, Mitts saw that he held something in his hand. And Mitts realised, with a degree of horror, that it was one of the screwdrivers he had tossed away.

The one which'd bounced off the bed.

And clattered down onto the floor.

Heinmein turned the screwdriver over in his hands as if it was some strange, alien artefact. He turned his head to Mitts. Stared long and hard at him. And then, without a word, he slipped the screwdriver into his pocket. He did his *plod-sweep* back out of the room.

The door clanged shut behind him.

And Mitts allowed himself to breathe again.

———

Mitts worked much more quickly this time.

With a little perspiration running down his face—he supposed that Heinmein, following his experimentation in Mitts's room had decided to turn up the thermostat—Mitts got three of the four screws loose from the ventilation hatch.

He placed them, carefully, in the pocket of his jeans.

Only one screw remaining, Mitts went at it as fast as he could, finding that, after undoing the other three, he had caught the knack.

With that one gone too, and stowed safely in his pocket, Mitts reached out and dug his fingertips in underneath the edges of the ventilation hatch.

Prying it open with his long fingernails.

It was another brief struggle, but Mitts eventually pulled the hatch loose.

Dust puffed up into the air.

As he bent down to lay the hatch on the plastic container, Mitts breathed the dust into his lungs. He felt it line his throat. He coughed it loose, waited a minute or so for the dust to clear from the air, and then he turned his attention upward once more.

To the now-open space in the wall.

His heart thudded hard in his throat, and in the under-side of his wrists, and up at his temples.

For a few moments, Mitts thought that he might lose consciousness.

That his mind might find some way of escaping him.

But he held himself steady.

Told himself to breathe in deeply to keep himself calm.

This was no time for him to lose his nut.

Mitts glanced off in the direction of his bedroom door, half expecting to hear another of Heinmein's knocks up against the metal. But there was no sound.

Not of footsteps, or of heavy breathing.

Or anything, for that matter.

Mitts glanced at the face of his wristwatch, saw that he had a good few hours or so before his father would *think* about calling him in for dinner.

That was all he needed.

Just a little time.

Mitts stepped up onto the plastic container, and then he reached up for the open space. He felt his hands reach inside. He tried to grip something within. He wanted to find something he could hang onto. Something he might be able to use to drag himself upward.

He thought back to being at school, to when he had gone to PE and passed by the gym: the one which was open to older kids and to the general public.

They had had one of those chin-up bars there, and Mitts could still recall observing those flabby-bodied, stay-at-home mothers, or else the beer-bellied widowed pensioners all red-faced and hauling themselves upward.

A couple of times, on his way past, Mitts had observed them through the steamed-up glass. He had watched as they managed maybe two or three repetitions on the chin-up bar.

Mitts would never give it a try himself—he didn't *need* to —he knew just from looking that he wouldn't have been able to manage so much as *one* repetition.

Not with *his* scrawny body.

But he had to try now.

His fingertips ran over the surface of what felt like a sturdy pipe.

He gripped hold of it.

Squeezed it.

Then, again sinking his teeth into his lower lip, he tensed all the muscles in his arms.

He pulled with all the strength he had.

Felt the soles of his trainers leaving the plastic container beneath him.

He managed to keep himself suspended in the air for ten seconds.

He knew because he counted them out in his mind.

But he couldn't tug himself up any further.

It just seemed impossible.

Mitts let go of whatever it was he clung to within the hatch.

His feet landed back down on the plastic container with a twin pair of *thuds*.

Feeling a tingle all over the surface of his body, he just stood there, breathing in the dust lingering in the air. And Heinmein's stench of rotten oranges and cheesy feet.

He stared back up at the ventilation hatch and told himself that, later, he would give it another go.

When he'd got his strength back.

———

In the evening, Mitts sat about the enormous kitchen table with his father.

Each of them on one of the towering stools.

The two of them were chomping on the spaghetti his father had prepared, and Mitts was just about losing his mind from the basil-flavoured tomato sauce which accompanied it.

What Mitts wouldn't have done for a light sprinkling of cheese. But there was little prospect of cheese until he could find his way out through the ventilation hatch.

Mitts managed to shake himself free of the thought of cheese when he saw Heinmein come skulking in for his portion of dinner.

Mitts's nostrils filled at the remembrance of that cheesy-feet stench which followed Heinmein around.

Even when he had slipped out of the kitchen again.

As he chewed away at his spaghetti, Mitts felt his whole body ache.

Not just his forearms like he would've thought.

His calves, all the way up to his thighs, and then his stomach, his shoulders.

Even the soles of his feet seemed to have been straining themselves.

He wondered if he'd been in such bad physical condition when he'd arrived to the Compound, or if he had got weedy during his time here.

Still, the aches and pains didn't dishearten him.

He knew his family's safety depended on him getting up into that hatch.

Even if it cost him his arm, he would do it.

Like always, Mitts got through with his dinner before his father had really started. Now that there were only two of them at the table for meals, he had only to give his father a wide-eyed look—and his father a dismissive nod—so that he was permitted to go fetch seconds from the pot.

When Mitts sat back down at the kitchen table, ready to

tuck into his second helping of spaghetti, he felt something overpowering within him.

It seemed so long since he had last seen his mother.

And it sent a slight pang to the base of his gut.

In all the silent hours which Mitts spent by himself— about the Compound, in his bedroom—he had had time to think. To think about just what sort of a life they all had here.

Hiding away from the outside world as if that would make things better.

Would they ever go outside again?

Mitts wanted to discuss his mother with his father, but he saw that his father seemed preoccupied.

His father stared down at his plate of spaghetti, pronging the odd strand here and there, but never really making progress.

Mitts saw that a single splash of red sauce had landed on the collar of his father's shirt.

He thought of telling him about the stain, but supposed that, in the end, his father would find out for himself.

That when it came time to wash his shirt, his father would see the stain and take care of it.

Although Mitts still had half his plate remaining, he didn't feel like having any more. He felt a touch nauseous, actually. He put it down to his exertion this afternoon.

Mitts laid his fork down on his metal plate with a slight *clang*. He looked back at his father.

"Mitts," his father said, his tone flat, "there's something I need to tell you."

Mitts felt his heart pump harder.

He felt the blood fizzle up to his brain.

His vision went a little fuzzy.

This sounded an *awful lot* like that day . . . the day when . . .

"It's about your mother," his father continued, "the reason why she's been in bed for so long."

Although Mitts tried his best not to show interest, to widen his eyes so much that his father might see the anxiety which gripped him, he couldn't help it.

"What?" he said. "What is it?"

His father broke off his gaze with Mitts and stared down at his emptied plate.

Next, he pressed his hands together, almost as if praying.

He jabbed his index fingers into the underside of his chin.

Mitts noticed the slight pulse in his father's throat, the gentle, almost undiscernible beating of the vein just beneath his skin.

Mitts breathed in the scent of buttery water which clung to the kitchen air. He could still taste the tomato-sauce flavour at the back of his throat, and would continue to do so for much of the night, he was sure.

"Your mother, we . . ." his father went on, and, as he did, Mitts noticed the slight film of tears in his father's eyes.

Mitts stared harder at the side of his father's face, wondering what he might be about to say next.

Were they going to leave? Was that what it was?

Or was it worse . . . had his mother's condition deteriorated?

Had Heinmein 'recommended' that his mother leave the Compound?

Mitts felt a tremor pass through his chest, but he forced himself to listen to his father's words.

When his father turned back to him, his eyes were red, and his cheeks had gone all puffy. It was almost as if he had had some sort of an allergic reaction to the sauce, or to the pasta, or *both*.

"You're going to have a little brother, or sister."

In that moment, Mitts felt his mind unstitching itself.

All at once, he felt as though he was high—*too high*—up from the ground.

For some reason, within his mind's eye, he pictured that he was surrounded by pointed, dark-purple hills.

Buffeting winds.

Winds which he couldn't possibly resist.

Not even if he'd been the strongest kid on Earth.

So he fell.

As she stepped away from the French doors, he felt a cool breeze blow against his face. He took another sip of champagne. Savoured the bitter taste. Felt the bubbles tickle his throat. Hang in his chest. He breathed in the hidden roses once again.

The string quartet fluttered away on the air. Never quite in range of hearing. Never designed to be heard out here, up on the balcony.

Her face was fresh, peachy, her cheeks slightly red as if she had pinched them to make them that way. She looked so much younger than she had seemed only moments ago. When they had stood inside the large hall, among all the others: the endless penguins, in their tuxedos; the endless birds-of-paradise, in their brightly coloured frocks and sparkly trimmings.

They had been just like any of the others.

Components of a larger universe.

Just a pair of twinkling stars.

Just as unique, and just as rare.

And equally commonplace.

He had expected her to follow. But, still, seeing her here now, it seemed strange.

Otherworldly.

She took another few steps forward.

Until she—like him—was lost to the dark.

A VISION OF HELL

Mitts *could hear the sirens wailing out.*
They dragged him awake.

Snagged his eyelids.

Peeled them open.

Rain pounding on the rooftops.

Its *scent* on the air.

He heard scurrying, about the house, someone screaming.

His mother?

A deeper voice, harder footsteps.

Mitts turned to his bedroom door.

It flew open.

His father stood there.

Barking instructions.

Instructions that simply couldn't be heard.

Not over the wailing sirens.

Mitts blinked himself around.

Felt his father's harsh grip on him.

Dragging him up and out of bed.

Telling him to *pack*.

Mitts could smell sulphur, too, amongst the rain.

He tasted ash in his mouth.

The house . . . was it burning down?

His father was gone.

Before he had the chance to ask.

Mitts hurried himself, matching his father's panic.

His whole body trembled, his mind still half seeped in sleep.

His heart hummed, up in his throat, unable to believe.

Mitts didn't pause to think. He only dragged the drawers open. He pawed about. For what he needed. For his clothes. A few books. He tossed everything he had into the sports bag he used for PE—throwing out his PE kit as he went.

He threw the bag strap over his shoulder.

He slipped out through his bedroom door.

Between the two of them, his parents lugged a hard-shelled suitcase.

One of those enormous, two-hundred-litre capacity ones they'd taken on a family trip to Australia, a few years before.

Dizzily, Mitts eyed the *Australian Air* tag which continued to cling to the handle of the suitcase.

Neither of his parents had thought to remove the tag either before or right now.

There was no time.

Mitts had no clue what was happening.

But there was no time.

Mitts followed his parents down the staircase, toward the front door. He felt some of the books he'd crammed into his sports bag jab him in the spine.

But he tried not to allow it to bother him.

He *couldn't* allow it to bother him.

Whatever was going on was a matter of life or death.

As Mitts descended the staircase, on his parents' heels, the smell of smoke grew stronger. He felt the ash layering itself into his lungs. He could feel his blood fizzle about his veins. And he wanted—more than *anything else*—to close his eyes and return to sleep.

Then this might all go away.

When Mitts crossed the threshold of their home, he heard himself calling out to his parents: the two of them already trotting across the driveway, headed for a battered, grey-blue estate car.

The car sat on the curb, idling, its exhaust puffing white smoke into the night-time air.

Its windscreen wipers slashing back and forth—*double-time*—attempting to keep the rain from completely covering the glass.

Mitts called out for the key.

So he might lock the front door.

But neither of his parents responded.

They lugged the bag between the two of them.

No time to use the wheels on the bottom to drag it along.

Mitts trudged after them, glancing back over his shoulder with each step, to the still wide-open front door of their home. Staring back into his house now, he saw that the welcoming, yellow light continued to shine.

Inviting him back in.

Inviting them *all* back in.

Back to their place of safety.

The rain drenched his clothes.

Hammered down on his head.

It drummed the car's metal roof.

Even as his parents loaded their suitcase into the back of the car, even as his father grabbed hold of Mitts's sports bag and threw it in too, he knew they would never be returning home.

Nobody had said anything.

Nobody had told Mitts what was going on.

But he knew.

He *just* knew.

That was all there was to it.

And then there was only the stench of cheesy feet.

Of rotten oranges.

Doctor Heinmein at the wheel.

Expressionless.

Driving Mitts away from all he had ever known.

Forever.

————

Mitts could hear their voices now.

Mumbling.

Garbled.

Mixing and fading.

One into the next.

When he crooked open an eye, the whole world which surrounded him was bleary. He breathed in and caught an aftertaste of the basil-flavoured tomato sauce.

And those same cheesy feet.

That sweet stench of rotten oranges.

His chest felt tight, and he could feel something clinging to his wrist.

He breathed in, trying to regain his senses.

And really knowing that he was helpless.

That he had been . . . rendered helpless.

When Mitts finally did get his eyes open all the way, when he managed to distinguish forms from the blindingly bright, white light, he realised that he was back in his bedroom.

The twitch of the springs in the camp-bed mattress beneath him.

The plastic container.

His wristwatch lying beside his bed.

He blinked again.

Trying to draw the scene clear.

Three figures—*three* of them.

One sat on the bed.

The other two hung back.

Just shadowy blurs for now.

But, with another few blinks, Mitts drew them clear.

He made out his mother and father.

His father supporting his mother.

Both of them with anxiety strewn across their features.

Anxiety for *him*.

He felt a warmth pass through his blood.

And then he turned his attention onto the foreground.

Onto Heinmein who perched on the edge of the mattress. His fingers coiled about Mitts's wrist. Taking his pulse.

Heinmein's palms were a touch sweaty.

He wanted Heinmein to release him.

But when Mitts looked beyond the ragged, white lab coat, and up into those black eyes, he couldn't help but see the determined drive staring right back at him.

The doctor counting out the beats of Mitts's heart within his mind.

Measuring Mitts's health, comparing it to whatever cold, hard statistics he used to keep tabs on human-life signs.

Finally, Heinmein released Mitts's wrist.

Heinmein retreated from the bed. Without another word to anybody, his clipboard dangling down from his fingers, he limped out of Mitts's bedroom.

Brought the metal door shut behind him with a distant *clang*.

Mitts turned his attention back to his parents. His brain still felt somewhat foggy. And he could feel a tingling sensation dancing its way all across his skin. He tried to sit up, but it was impossible, he only slunk back down onto the camp-bed mattress.

Felt the springs jutting into his spine.

Someone—his mother . . . his father?—had dressed him in his pyjamas.

When Mitts looked up again, both his parents were staring down at him.

Both of them wearing looks of deep concern on their faces.

He took in his mother's face.

He caught sight of her black hair, cropped back to the nape of her neck. She wore a nightgown, as if Mitt's father had only just roused her from sleep.

Mitts's father wore the shirt, as he had before. That splodge of tomato sauce still there, as yet uncleaned.

Mitts saw how those dark circles continued to cling to the bases of his mother's eye sockets. That her eyeballs were webbed with red veins. She seemed to have grown thin, just as Mitts had.

He wished there might be something he could do for her.

Something he could do to help her condition.

But, feeling his energy waning once more, he knew he didn't even have enough strength to help himself.

If only he'd been bigger.

If only he'd been born stronger.

Then maybe . . . *maybe* . . .

Mitts looked to his father, standing to his left, and then to his mother, who had taken up a position on his right. He thought back on what his father had said; the last thing he remembered.

In the kitchen.

That puff of buttery steam from the pot.

The crippling nausea which'd gripped him.

How he'd slipped from the stool and fell.

Right . . .

. . . Down.

It'd all gone black.

Or had it?

Mitts recalled something, some sort of a . . . *another world?*

Those dark-purple hills.

That buffeting wind.

And then . . . darkness.

Mitts realised his parents were speaking to him.

Slowly, their voices made sense.

At first, they were as indiscernible as the beating of birds' wings.

Mitts had to concentrate.

He screwed up his forehead.

His father's voice; first, thick and gruff, came to him.

". . . How're . . . feeling?"

Mitts tried to nod back to his father, but, in that second, he was blindsided by an overwhelming migraine. It ripped through his brain.

Laid waste to what might've been rational thoughts.

Rational words.

In the end, Mitts heard himself groan.

He felt his mother's cool touch against his cheek.

It calmed him.

Slowed his swiftly beating heart.

He turned to her now.

Feeling the creeping, tingling sensation all through his blood, Mitts tried his best to clear his mind. To bring his mother clear. But her features continued to blur.

He made out her lips.

Distinguished words.

At last.

One long string of clarity.

"Doctor Heinmein," she said, "he will be back in a few moments, with some medicine, something that will help."

Mitts couldn't quite recall if Heinmein entered his bedroom then . . . or if it happened several minutes later.

But the world, soon after, was lost in a cacophony of sulphur-smelling chemicals.

And dreary, drug-induced sleep.

———

Mitts woke feeling a chill.

It was like those mornings, back home, in early September. The time in the year just before his parents would switch on the central heating. Sometimes Mitts would wake up shuddering, almost unable to breathe, from the cold of the night.

He would pry himself up out of bed, shove his duvet off him and go fetch his black, fleecy jumper out of his chest of drawers.

Then he would tug his duvet back up and shiver himself into some sort of a light sleep until the brightening morning woke him later.

On those mornings, he always asked his mother to make hot chocolate for breakfast.

He remembered, feeling the bags tugging at the bases of his eye sockets, how he would peer down into his swirling cup; breathing in the gentle, smooth odour of chocolate, feeling it channel warmth back into his bones as if it was some kind of elixir.

When Mitts glanced about the room—the room within the Compound where he was now—he saw that it was dark, all except for a single light source.

It took him a couple of moments to figure out it was a torch.

A sickly, yellow circle of light illuminated a shadowy corner of the room.

It was strange, now, to see anything that wasn't rendered by the striking, too-bright *white* fluorescent lights of the Compound.

There was something almost *natural* about the torchlight.

Mitts lifted himself a little up off his spring-loaded, camp-bed mattress.

The springs creaked out beneath him.

He could tell there was a person sitting there—slumped—resting upon his plastic container. He realised the plastic container had been moved away from its previous position just below the ventilation hatch.

He wondered if anybody: his mother, his father, Hein-mein might've taken a look inside.

If they had then surely they would've discovered the screwdrivers there.

Perhaps somebody had noticed the screwdrivers had gone missing from the maintenance cupboard. Even though Mitts had gone out of his way to snatch the screwdrivers from a little-used cupboard, he couldn't help feeling that—somehow —fate might've conspired against him.

Made it so he simply wouldn't be allowed to get away with what it was he hoped to achieve.

The figure slumped up in the corner. He held a book in his hand.

The figure aimed a glance at him.

Mitts finally recognised his father's profile.

How his father had his sleeves rolled up.

His father, still in silhouette, folded the page of his book and laid it down carefully on top of the plastic container. Then he trod on over to Mitts.

As he drew closer, as Mitts used the torchlight to read his father's face, he saw his eyelids were drooping. Like his mother, his father had black bags beneath his eye sockets.

Even how he had approached the bed, he could tell that his father's energy was depleted, that his shoulders sagged, that his gait dragged.

Mitts wondered if the Compound had sapped his father's strength.

As it had sapped his own.

His father perched down lightly on the edge of the mattress.

Mitts heard the springs within his camp bed slink back and forth.

His father reached forward and laid his hand across Mitts's forehead. "How're you feeling?" he said.

Mitts tried to swallow, but felt as if something blocked his throat.

When he tried to cough it loose, he rendered himself unable to breathe.

It was only with his father's help that he was eventually able to sit upright in bed.

Mitts looked to his father, feeling his eyes streaming with

tears from the effort of trying to clear his throat. Mitts's chest tickled and he could feel a tightening sensation over his veins. Although Mitts had never wanted to as a kid—back when he'd been carefree, and they'd lived at home—he now had a seemingly irrepressible desire to go run through a park somewhere.

Just rush back and forth, grinning all over.

Feeling the tickle of oxygen flowing into his lungs.

Bringing him back to life.

But that life was gone now.

The Compound was all that remained.

Just Mitts and his mother, and his father.

Having got his coughing fit under some sort of control, and trying to ease his weary body, he looked to his father.

His father attempted a smile, but it withered and died upon his lips.

He looked away from Mitts, as if he couldn't bear to look him in the eye.

As if it was all it would take to set things right again, Mitts reached out and grasped hold of his father's thigh. He gave it a squeeze. "I'm . . . I'm okay, Dad," Mitts got out.

But, the truth was, Mitts felt very far from 'okay'.

In fact, even right then, he could feel the swirling nausea returning to him.

And there was nothing he could do.

Except lie himself down.

Stare up at the ceiling.

And wish it away.

———

The next time Mitts woke, he realised that he'd been dreaming about those dark-purple hills.

About the buffeting winds.

And he had smelled that sulphuric odour, all around him.

On his clothes.

In his mouth.

In his *lungs*.

His mouth tasted of pill capsules: that plasticky, *nothing* taste.

He could hear a light *hum* in his ears.

When Mitts looked about himself, still feeling those pinpricks of pain from the coughing fit who knew how many hours ago, he realised that the main light in his room was illuminated.

That, once more, the bright, white light had returned.

That meant it was daytime.

Heinmein had put the lights in the entire Compound on a timer so that it might emulate the day.

But the sun was one thing, and artificial light was another.

And Mitts couldn't say that he felt any the better for the bright, white light which streamed through the room.

Now, though, Mitts was alone.

He looked across the room, to the plastic container, where

his father had been sat. The torch was still there, lying on top of it. And the book his father had been reading was there too.

Mitts breathed in deeply. He wondered if he had the strength—if he *still* had the strength—to hoik himself up. To set himself on his own two feet.

There was only one way to find out.

He had to try.

Mitts shovelled off his blanket—easier to summon the strength than he had imagined—and he eased his body over to the edge of his camp bed.

The slipping and sliding of the springs beneath him sent jitters through his body.

He so wished that they would be silent.

He recalled his bed back home, when he could easily move around without making so much as a sound. That time was *gone*, though . . . no point wondering after the past . . .

Now at the edge of his bed, Mitts summoned the strength to dangle his legs, to have his toenails scrape the laminate flooring.

He glanced up to his bedroom door, half expecting to see either his mother or father there, looking on.

With some vacant expression on their face.

But there was no one.

He was alone.

Somewhat heartened by his efforts so far, Mitts used the metal frame of his camp bed to help himself up onto the soles of his feet. Still holding the metal frame, he felt his balance come and go, as if he hadn't stood for weeks rather than a matter of hours.

Finally, he caught the courage to stand by himself.

Though he didn't feel one-hundred-percent natural standing on his own two feet, he could keep himself more or less still.

That was the important thing.

Just stand up.

All for now.

After what must've been a minute, Mitts eased himself along past his camp bed, headed for the door of his bedroom. Although he had no destination in mind beyond that, he couldn't help but make it his goal. It was only when he'd got about halfway across his bedroom floor that he realised he had a strong urge to urinate.

He glanced toward the en-suite bathroom, realising he would need to make a detour.

It took him the best part of what must've been a minute to reach it.

When he got done in there, he realised he could hear voices out in the corridor.

Outside his bedroom.

Still standing in the bathroom, Mitts concentrated his hearing onto those people, trying to separate the voices into identities.

He recognised one voice as belonging to his father.

Feeling that same queasiness coming on—that same *giddy*

sensation—Mitts blinked several times, managing to clear it away as best he could.

As his father's voice droned on—Mitts could make no sense of the words—he realised that he must be out in the corridor with Heinmein.

Mitts held his ground, wanting to see where this conversation was headed. But he realised, from where he stood, there would be very little he could make out distinctly.

So he headed back to his bed.

He slumped down.

Sent the springs of the camp-bed mattress creaking all over again.

Mitts drew his blanket back over himself, only then realising he was wearing the black fleece he would often put on for those unexpectedly cold early mornings.

He supposed either his mother or father had decided he needed the extra warmth and had dressed him in it.

Mitts could still hear his father's juddering voice in the one-way conversation. He willed it to stop. It was almost as if every word his father spoke was a hammer pounding his skull.

He could feel the giddiness returning.

Perhaps it had been a mistake for him to get up out of bed.

But he had gone and done it.

Too late for regrets . . .

Outside, Mitts was aware that the conversation had come to a halt.

Neither his father or Heinmein spoke.

Mitts could hear the sound of footsteps—of that *sweep-plod*—heading away from his bedroom.

There was a pair of—almost apologetic—knocks up against his metal bedroom door.

And then the hinges creaked.

Mitts's father appeared there.

He was dressed in a clean shirt now.

If Mitts hadn't known it was a new day from the fluorescent strip lights powering on, he would've known it from his father's lime-green, chequered shirt; the sleeves rolled up just above the elbows.

He wore the same loafers and jeans as the day before.

Or, at least, Mitts believed he did.

His father held one of the metal bowls from the kitchen. That was strange in itself seeing that his father was the mouthpiece for Mitts never—*ever*—eating outside the kitchen.

As his father approached, things got blurry again, but Mitts managed to keep his brain together.

To keep reality somewhat present before his eyes.

"Dad?" Mitts managed to get out.

If his father smiled, Mitts didn't see it.

Just like before, his father perched down on the edge of his camp bed. He passed the bowl toward him, and said, "Good to see you're awake."

Mitts raised a smile, then took the bowl. He saw that it

was cereal with powdered milk. He didn't like cereal at the best of times, and much less with *powdered* milk, but he felt strangely ravenous.

He seized hold of the spoon and dug in.

Only when Mitts had got about three quarters of the way through his cereal, and he looked up at his father, did he note the extreme concern in his face. How his father's eyes seemed almost as if they were strung with hair-triggers, and that they were scoping out every one of Mitt's movements as if any one might be his last.

Mitts tried to smile but found himself shaking almost uncontrollably.

It was a challenge for him to finish the cereal.

But he did.

He handed the bowl back to his father.

The two of them sat on the edge of the camp bed for a long time. Mitts realised he could hear the strangest of sounds. Coming from his father's throat. A sort of croaking sound. Like his father was trying as hard as he could to keep something inside.

In the end, Mitts decided to break the silence.

"Dad?" he said.

His father remained detached, staring into the air right before his nose, still clutching the cereal bowl. His hands were shaking lightly.

Mitts could see that—in the process of bringing the bowl

of cereal here—his father had spilled a little milk on the belly of his shirt.

Mitts continued, "I've been having dreams, strange dreams."

His father continued to stare out in front.

Apparently distracted by something which Mitts would never be able to see.

"It's a dream about a man—and a woman—and it's New Year's Eve, and they're standing up on a balcony, with the sounds of a string quartet in the background, and it's all dark . . . and then . . ."

In a single, swift, *violent* gesture, his father arced back his arm and tossed the metal cereal bowl hard against the wall.

———

The bowl bounced back with a metal *clatter*.

It tumbled down to the laminate flooring.

The spoon tinkled as it landed.

And then, all of a sudden, everything was still.

Everything was quiet.

Mitts stared in horror at the bowl.

Stared at the large dent in its rim.

Mitts could feel his cereal returning up his throat with a burning sensation.

But he swallowed it back.

He tasted those oats one more time, and the sour flavour of the powdered milk there too.

When he breathed in, he noticed the air stunk strongly of disinfectant.

Of radiation.

His father sat still for a very long time, staring in front of himself, clutching his knees as tightly as—*it seemed*—he could possibly manage.

Mitts felt a quick, uncontrollable tension seize his chest. His breaths came in gasps. When he examined his father's face in profile, he saw that he was mouthing along something.

That he was speaking words.

Words which Mitts was never meant to hear.

It wasn't until after a little while that Mitts's father seemed to remember Mitts was there at all.

When his father did, he turned his head around and looked closely at Mitts. "I've been thinking about how to . . ." his father lost his stream of thought for a moment then continued, ". . . what I should say so that it's clear so that to a . . . to a *child* it should be clear."

But Mitts thought that he already knew.

Mitts swallowed hard, making sure his cereal wouldn't make another reappearance, and then said, "I'm going to die, aren't I?"

His father didn't seem to hear him at all, he just continued to stare into nothingness.

Finally, his father stiffened slightly, turned to meet Mitts's eye, and said, "Yes."

His voice cracked about the edges, but the word was spoken strongly enough to be understood.

The two of them sat for a long while in silence.

For so long that Mitts wondered if his father even recalled that Mitts was there.

If his father recalled that *either* of them were there at all.

"Dad?" Mitts said.

No response.

"There's something else too," Mitts continued, "something else, along with those dreams, of the man and the woman."

Again, his father gave no indication of having heard.

But Mitts knew that he needed to tell him.

"When I fell from the stool," Mitts said, "from between the time when I fell off and the time that I hit the floor, and blacked out, I saw *things* . . . there was . . . I don't know how to explain it . . . some sort of . . . *different* place."

Mitts studied his father's face for any sign that he might've heard a word of what he had just said.

But his father just kept on staring. Apparently none the wiser.

"These dark-purple hills," Mitts went on, "these *winds*, really strong winds."

His father sniffed a couple of times.

His shoulders shook a touch and then, all at once, buckled completely.

His father crumpled over himself, his hands rushing up to cover his face.

But Mitts could still see the tears creep out from between his father's fingers.

Mitts wanted to be able to say something to reassure him, to tell him that everything was going to be okay, to have him *stop* what he was doing, but, at the same time, he knew that there *was* nothing he could say, nothing he could do.

Because, soon enough, Mitts wouldn't exist any longer.

He would return to . . . wherever it was he had come from in the first place.

The two of them sat like that, with his father crumpled up over himself, and Mitts wrapped up in his blankets, shaking all over.

Mitts wondered if someone might come along to interrupt them.

If his mother might appear in the doorway.

But Mitts knew his mother was too sick to come and see him.

That she had another child to take care of.

The one inside her belly.

Smelling the salt of his father's tears on the stilted air of his bedroom, and feeling the warmth slipping out through the surface of his skin, Mitts wanted to tell his father all about his dreams.

All about those visions he'd been having.

About those purple hills.

Those cutting winds.

But his father wouldn't hear him.

Not now.

Mitts could see that.

With the taste of the oats from his cereal still in his mouth, and the smell of that slightly sour-flavoured powdered milk thick in his nostrils, Mitts managed to keep his voice clear and straight, and directed at his father, "Dad?"

His father didn't react.

"How long have I got?"

Nothing from his father.

Mitts thought he might have to repeat his question.

But he didn't think he had the strength.

And then, quivering, and reedy, but *there*, his father replied, ". . . Doctor Heinmein, he thinks . . . thinks you might have about a week."

Mitts breathed in deeply, neither really absorbing the words or the true depth of their meaning.

He gave a nod, unseen by his father.

A week.

He could get *a lot* done in a week.

———

About half an hour later, there was a knock on Mitts's bedroom door.

Those twin *clangs* of human knuckles on metal.

Heinmein appeared there, in the doorway.

Feeling a little more clear-headed, Mitts reached out and gave his father a prod in his upper arm.

His father, apparently having drifted off, stirred with a slight mumble.

He seemed to recall where he was.

He blinked away his daze.

Looked over to the doorway.

He got to his feet, allowing Heinmein to take up his position on the camp bed.

As Mitts looked over Heinmein, he saw that he had brought a serrated metal case with him.

Heinmein laid the case across his lap.

For some reason, Mitts's hatred for Heinmein—for the man who'd taken them away from their home—faded somewhat.

He almost took the man in with cool detachment.

Almost as if Mitts could *pretend* that he didn't smell those cheesy feet of his, or that rotten stench of oranges.

Couldn't *taste* those things in his mouth.

Feel them suffocating him.

Heinmein popped open the case, and Mitts examined the contents.

The interior of the case was lined with a gunmetal-grey foam, separated into compartments.

Each compartment held a tiny glass vial or else a metallic component.

As Heinmein popped the pieces out of their places and assembled them with expert precision, he appeared to cast off the shell of his previously detached personality. "It shouldn't hurt," Heinmein said, "I have spent the time in the past few hours perfecting the dosage, creating a bespoke formula based on your own blood."

Mitts just nodded, feeling detached from the scene.

It had taken the most part of his strength to speak to his father. About his dreams. About the *visions*. Now he was paying the price.

So Mitts just sat still.

Like a good boy.

Heinmein constructed what Mitts recognised to be a syringe.

He filled it with a light-orange liquid from one of the glass vials.

He turned to Mitts, looked into his eyes.

And, even then, in that moment, Mitts realised even Heinmein's black eyes couldn't hold him at a distance any longer.

Mitts had some feeling inside, one which he would never be able to shake.

The feeling told him he needed to trust Heinmein now . . . if not ever again.

Mitts glanced over Heinmein's shoulder, to the door, to where his father stood.

His father propped himself against the wall, chewing on his knuckles.

Just staring into mid-air as he had done earlier.

How could Mitts expect his father to understand?

How could his father *know* what it might be like?

To see these things in his own mind, and so *clearly?*

But some things, Mitts supposed, could never be explained.

Having prepped everything that needed to be prepped, Heinmein examined the syringe.

Flicked the needle.

"This," Heinmein continued, stone-faced, and looking Mitts in the eye, "needs to go into your spine."

With a slight nod to Heinmein, Mitts turned his back.

He waited for the sharp, puncturing pain.

————

For the first few hours following the dosage, Mitts could hardly sit in one place. He felt too restless to do anything other than tread back and forth, burning off energy.

It felt like his blood was fizzing.

He could almost hear it gurgle through his ears.

Heinmein had asked Mitts to think of a fire, to think about the difference between a blazing fire and one which smouldered along; quietly crackling every now and again.

Mitts had felt like he was back in school.

As if he'd been kidnapped for some elementary chemistry lesson.

But he had paid attention to Heinmein.

Put those smells of rotten oranges and cheesy feet out of his mind.

The point which Heinmein had been trying to make with the fire was that when fire burns more strongly—*more brightly* —it uses up a larger amount of fuel.

Before Heinmein had gone, he had made it quite clear to Mitts—said it in so many ways; and so many different terms— that what he had administered him was not a cure. That there was no hope of Mitts getting better. And that, now Mitts had been given this injection, he would have another week's worth of full strength life.

And then, one day, sometime next week, he would drop dead.

Heinmein had clicked his fingers to get across *that* point.

Mitts recalled looking across the room, at that precise moment, and seeing his father flinch at Heinmein clicking his fingers.

For all he knew, Mitts had flinched too.

Mitts lay on his side, a position he never found comfortable to sleep in. He rubbed at the spot on his spine where

Heinmein had given him the injection. He could feel a welt there; a seemingly ever-growing lump. When he placed his fingertips over the form of it, he could feel his heart beating through an obtrusive vein.

He almost thought he could feel the serum—or whatever Heinmein had called it—billowing through his bloodstream.

Heinmein had told Mitts to expect to feel weak for a long while. For perhaps several hours. As the serum took hold, Mitts would feel as if someone had blown air into his lungs.

As if he had been brought back to life.

Right now, though, all Mitts felt was the need to sleep.

He could still sense his father, slumped over on the plastic container in the corner, reading the book by torchlight. His eyes mechanically wandering over the black lines, processing them all—and even Mitts could see this—without so much as a single one entering his consciousness.

When Mitts came around again, he felt an odd prickling sensation, all through his body. As if he had a battalion of sewing needles all attempting to poke themselves out through the surface of his skin. He itched at the welt on his spine, felt that the swelling had diminished a good deal. He unfurled an arm. Reached out for his wristwatch, lying beside his bed.

It'd just gone three a.m.

That would explain the darkness.

Mitts glanced about the room, taking in the shapes. He stared over into the corner, where the plastic container sat, and he waited for his eyes to adapt to the gloom.

Soon, he saw that his father was no longer there, that he had left his book lying, face down, its pages splayed, on the container. The narrow outline of the torch was there too.

Mitts turned his attention back inward, to that prickling sensation.

He itched at all the places on his skin which felt like they needed itching.

But new itches would spring up elsewhere.

No matter how much he scratched.

It might've been an hour before Mitts finally felt the sensation leave him. When he no longer felt that prickle frustratingly just below the surface of his skin. He peeled off his blankets, used his bathroom, and then trod about his bedroom, experimenting.

Just as Heinmein had said, the dizziness—the *nausea*—had gone now, and Mitts could see perfectly straight, albeit only into the darkness.

When Mitts thought about it, he realised that the prickling sensation had retreated, but hadn't entirely disappeared. It had been replaced by a throbbing. This sense that something, within his blood, was now giving him warmth. It was resonating with a sort of *energy*, pouring it directly into his skin.

Mitts had the urge to run.

He wanted to burn off some energy.

He felt so alert.

After brushing his fingertips over the welt on his spine,

Mitts eased himself out through his bedroom door. Bare-footed, he gazed up and down the corridor—lit with an eerie, imitation-twilight glow.

He picked a direction.

Beat one foot after the next.

He took paces larger than he ever would've thought himself capable.

————

Mitts returned to his bedroom. He felt the sweat ooze out of his skin. His heart wouldn't sit still. It continued its merry jig against his ribs. Not content to allow him any rest.

He sniffed at the air.

There . . . there it was again.

That odour.

Disinfectant.

The one which he had reported to Heinmein earlier . . . the one which his father had *forced* him to report to Heinmein.

Mitts thought back to how Heinmein had administered the dose. All things considered, he had really been quite caring. Perhaps Heinmein wasn't as bad as he'd thought.

Maybe, because Mitts was dying, their relationship had thawed.

If Mitts cropped up in the doorway of Heinmein's office, maybe Heinmein would acknowledge him.

Ask him what the matter was.

Just because Mitts was dying, didn't mean he could forget about protocol.

Protocol was what had kept his family alive thus far.

But what would Heinmein do?

Even if—and that *was* a big if—Heinmein deigned to come and check out Mitts's bedroom, it would only be for him to bring along that device of his, the one which emitted the electronic *groans* and *whirrs*.

Heinmein would screw up his eyes, staring at the dial. And then, a few minutes later, he would trudge on out of Mitts's bedroom, leaving Mitts none the wiser.

Not even bothering to tell him whether or not there was anything to be worried about.

Mitts turned his attention up toward the ventilation hatch.

He glanced down at his wristwatch.

Saw that it was a few minutes past half four in the morning.

His father would be knocked out—*comatose*.

He had been up caring for Mitts for so long. He wouldn't stir until the lighting system gently woke him. Mitts had until sometime between seven and seven thirty.

So Mitts had the time, and, he believed, the strength, to investigate for himself.

He had to take his chance now. He would be dead next week.

Mitts turned his attention to the plastic container on the other side of the room. He looked to his father's book, its pages all splayed.

Then he glanced to the torch.

He snatched it up. Slipped it into the waistband of his pyjama bottoms.

Then he dragged the plastic container across the floor.

Left it beneath the ventilation hatch.

He stood back from his work, thought about what he was doing.

Wondered if it *was* the right thing.

But then, what was he meant to do now?

There was nobody to tell him either way.

Right *or* wrong.

Mitts cracked open the lid of the plastic container.

He dug about inside.

He cast aside clothing, books, other assorted oddities he had dragged along with him to the Compound. He located the screwdrivers.

They were where he'd left them.

Stuffed into a pair of socks.

The fact that they were still there, in his container, suggested that no one had uncovered them.

Or, at least, nobody had thought there was anything untoward about him having them.

Mitts leaped up onto the plastic container, feeling invigorated now.

As if his whole body might shudder from the shock of the new energy burning through him.

Flipping on the torch and then laying it at his feet, Mitts reached up, undid the loosened screws from the ventilation hatch, one by one. He dropped each, in succession, onto his camp bed.

Taking extreme care, Mitts peeled back the ventilation hatch itself.

He laid it down on the laminate flooring, just beside the plastic container.

It would be easy to find when he returned.

That done, Mitts gazed about his bedroom, half expecting to see either his father, or mother, or Heinmein standing in the doorway.

But nobody was there.

He was all alone.

In the dark.

———

Mitts lay on his front. He could feel the cool metal, even through his fleecy top, and through his pyjama bottoms.

As he crawled his way along the air vent, he could hear his hands and feet making muted *booms* against the metal.

It smelled strongly of ammonium—what Mitts had *learned* was the smell of ammonium.

It caught at the back of his throat, leaving an almost fishy taste.

But even the smell of ammonium was overwhelmed by the odour of disinfectant now.

Mitts was still surprised that he had managed to haul himself up into the air vent.

When he had seized hold of the tube, he had been convinced that there would be precisely zero chance of him being able to sustain himself.

And then there'd been the doubts about whether or not the tube would hold.

But it had.

Mitts could still recall his distant surprise as he had brought himself up level with the opening of the air vent. And he bet that it was that same surprise which had given him the kick he needed to *keep on* tugging himself on into the vent.

And so, here he was now.

After about five metres, there had been a junction in the air vent.

He could've chosen left, or right.

When he had shone the torch off down either route, he had observed the gentle bend of the vent to the left, seen that it was headed back toward the Restricted Area.

That wouldn't be any good.

No good at all.

At the back of his mind, he wished it'd been raining hard. Like it had been several nights ago.

When he had smelled that strong scent of disinfectant before.

So he would know which way led to the surface.

But, as it turned out, Mitts had had to make a snap judgement.

To turn right.

And so, here he was now.

He was heading up a gentle incline.

When he'd first come up against the slope, he had worried that it might become so acute as to prove impossible to navigate.

That, as he climbed up—further and further—he would lose his grip and slide back down.

Then all this would've been in vain.

But Mitts kept on going.

And the slope held steady.

Mitts supposed that he'd been crawling for about fifteen minutes when he first felt the change in air temperature.

Hot.

So hot.

Almost instantly, it caused him to sweat.

His palms, as they crawled their way along the air vent, slipped out from beneath him.

Unable to grip any longer.

But he pressed himself forward, hoping the temperature would fluctuate.

That the gentle air conditioning which he was so accustomed to might return.

But, if anything, the temperature rose.

Mitts, though, had no intention of giving up.

He hauled himself along, feeling every single kilo of his body.

Only when he thought to turn his torch off did he realise that he wasn't in darkness.

That there was light entering the air vent.

Daylight.

Mitts glanced about him, seeing the different vents, branching off into different rooms within the Compound. Above and beyond the Restricted Area.

He peered through a few of them, saw the deserted offices.

The cleared desks.

The unoccupied furniture.

For some strange reason, it made him feel sad.

This ebbing, *rippling* sadness which seemed to hollow him out from within.

Turn his guts to a cool, revolting goo.

There would never be people in these offices.

Never again.

His parents might think that Mitts was nothing but a dumb kid.

But he had caught onto more than they might've imagined.

He carried on his way, telling himself where he needed to go.

There was only one acceptable destination.

He wanted to see where the rain came from.

After five minutes more of crawling, he got there.

To a much larger ventilation hatch.

One with several more screws keeping it held in place.

Mitts hadn't brought the screwdriver along with him. In any case, he doubted his ability—even with his renewed strength—to loosen all those screws before his father got up out of bed.

Let alone pry the hatch itself off.

But Mitts could see out through the fins, the ones which angled downward, to the ground. He pushed his face up against the hatch. He peered through. Trying to see something.

Anything.

Some remainder of the world.

Of the *real* world.

All Mitts could see, though, was grey.

Beaten-up asphalt.

Abandoned parking bays marked out in white paint.

Puddles of grey rainwater.

Undisturbed.

Mitts listened hard.

Tried to hear *something*.

He wished to hear birds chirping.

Perhaps a peal of thunder, announcing a coming storm.

Something to remind him that he inhabited a living, breathing—*bleeding*—world.

But there was nothing at all.

Not a sound.

Just the eerie, ever-lasting stillness.

Mitts breathed in deeply. He tried to catch some of the smell of disinfectant.

But he couldn't.

No matter how hard he strained himself.

How hard he implored his brain to pick it out from the cold odour of damp gravel and mud.

Mitts was ready to turn away from the outside world. He knew his father would soon be stirring.

He would be coming to check up on him.

Wouldn't it be a shock for him to find his son gone?

For a few moments, Mitts played with that imagining.

His father happening upon his bedroom, upon Mitts's empty camp bed.

What would be his father's range of emotions?

He would be distraught, of course.

Perhaps he would risk tapping the red button to open the Restricted Area blast doors.

Maybe he would put the rest of them in peril.

Put his mother in peril.

No, Mitts couldn't allow himself to be responsible for that.

He needed to return to his camp bed.

He needed to return to the Restricted Area.

As Mitts turned away from the ventilation hatch, something caught his eye.

Later, when he thought about it, he was sure his imagination plugged in many of the details.

Grey-purple skin.

Saucer-shaped, beady black eyes.

Spiderlike fangs.

Gooey spittle hanging down from them.

And then, the overwhelming stench of sulphur.

More than anything—more than *anything else*—Mitts wanted to scream.

He wanted to use all his strength to scream harder than he ever had before.

But he could not.

The soft night closed in on the two of them.

He could feel the warmth emanating from her body.

Her skin fragile as a rose petal.

And her body slick, well-synchronised with this world.

No stranger to its devices.

The silk of her dress up against his skin. The bubbles of champagne easing their way down his throat. The dryness it left in his mouth as the alcohol took with it his saliva. All moisture.
Left him gagging with thirst.

Now that they could no longer see one another, it was hard to tell where each of them began, where each one ended. And it occurred to him that it didn't matter any longer. That whatever fiction he told himself—whatever lies he said—that was all they would be.

Because they would be designed for one purpose, and one purpose only.

To conceal reality.

He felt her draw close now.

Close enough that he might reach out and touch her.

But he was afraid . . . so afraid . . . and so she made the first move.

Her lips were warm and moist up against his earlobe as she whispered, "Five minutes to midnight."

PART 2
SAM AMERICA

The air was heavy with ash.

It fluttered down like light snowfall.

Layered down over the loose stones of the beach. And onto the surface of the steel-grey waves. Whether the water reflected the sky, or vice versa, was a matter for debate.

And one which, quite frankly, had lost all meaning.

Sam America could feel his muscles rippling beneath his white cotton shirt. His woolly hair twirled in the sulphur-stinking breeze. White stars speckled his Yankee-blue waistcoat. Confederate-red clung to the stripes of his trousers, and to his suspenders.

He wore a pair of bulky, ankle-high boots.

His hat—red-and-white vertical stripes up the crown; white stars on a blue background about the band—had blown away hours ago.

Somehow—for some reason—Sam America felt naked without his hat.

Almost as if he might be a post-apocalyptic Samsun.

Sheered of his strength.

But, deep down, Sam America knew that he still possessed his strength, and, more to the point, that it would never leave him.

Because what the world needed now—what it most needed right now—was a hero.

SEVEN YEARS

When Mitts *woke* to the sound of a child's cries, he was confused.

Eyes still closed, he reached up and rubbed at his temples.

He padded about himself, trying to clarify his location.

His camp bed.

Beneath him.

That familiar *creak-creak* of springs.

Beneath his weight.

The smells of baking wafted in beneath his bedroom door. He caught the scent of butter and flour.

He could already feel his mouth watering.

When Mitts opened his eyes, he realised that the bright fluorescent lights were operating at full power. It was morning. Perhaps *mid*-morning if his judgement could be trusted.

The battery in his wristwatch had finally run out a couple of weeks ago so he could never be one-hundred-per-cent certain of the exact time.

Today he turned eighteen years old.

He didn't need a wristwatch to know that.

Seven years.

In the Compound.

In the Restricted Area.

He propped himself up on the mattress of his camp bed, still lost in a dream . . . of that superhero, or whatever the hell he had been . . .

He thought back to the moment when his father had told him that he was going to die—that he would be dead within a week.

That was the last time Mitts had attempted to share his dreams with anybody.

Before, it had been the dancers.

Before that, visions of the hills.

Over his years in the Compound, Mitts had learned that each one of them needed to find their own way of coping with being encased within their own mind.

Mitts had never thought—*not for one second*—of telling anyone what had happened that early morning. When he had crawled through the air vents.

When he had come up against that . . . that *creature* . . .

And yet, Mitts was certain it was the encounter with the

creature which explained *why* he hadn't died a week after the dosage; as Heinmein had expected.

Mitts thought about how he'd felt Heinmein's eyes lock onto him a week following the administration of the serum. It was like Heinmein had been holding up a test tube, patiently waiting for the liquid within to change its colour, so that it might confirm a hypothesis.

But Mitts had refused to change colour.

He had stayed the same.

He had *got better*.

Once a month had gone by, and Mitts still hadn't died, Heinmein had begun to carry out experiments.

At first, these had taken the form of an extended weekly medical check-up.

Mitts had no doubt Heinmein had designed his approach to be subtle, so that his parents wouldn't suspect. That Heinmein was merely doing all he could to *ensure* their son was fully cured.

But, soon enough, it had been impossible for Heinmein to hide his intent.

Following one of the weekly medical check-ups, Heinmein had insisted he be committed to one of the examination rooms. Heinmein had wanted to hook him up to all sorts of machines. To display all of Mitts's bodily functions neatly on neon-lit monitors.

That was the first time his father said *no*.

Even now—even seven years later—Mitts could still feel

the swelling sensation in his chest as his father faced off with Heinmein.

When he had analysed it afterwards, he knew just what the feeling represented:

Pride.

After that, Heinmein had taken special care *not* to pay Mitts more than his due attention during the weekly medical check-ups.

After a few months, Heinmein seemed to forget entirely about the matter.

If possible, Heinmein had become more reclusive.

Only ever leaving his office for food once every few days, rather than several times a day, as had been his routine.

Not that Mitts was complaining.

Not in the slightest.

Because, despite the years, his opinion toward Heinmein had not shifted.

He blamed him.

Distrusted him.

He knew it was his responsibility—*his responsibility alone* —to keep an eye on Heinmein.

But everything changed several months later.

Mitts's mother gave birth.

Mitts slept through the entire experience.

When he went to the kitchen the next morning, he recalled seeing his father. He had been shaking all over. His complexion bone-white as he gripped a cup of black coffee.

His parents named the baby Fluva, and though Mitts wasn't sure about *that* name, or his own, to be honest, he said nothing about it.

He had seen all those photos his parents thought they hid so carefully, at the back of their wardrobe. That album of yellowing, faded photographs in which his parents were decked out in all sorts of hippywear:

Tie-dye t-shirts.

Flares.

Wide-collared shirts.

Long hair.

Purple-tinted sunglasses.

. . . All those mysteries they had thought they kept secret.

Fluva—or 'Floo', as she became known throughout the Compound—took an extreme liking to Heinmein.

Mitts recalled the first few days after Floo had learned how to walk. Heinmein would come skulking into the kitchen, at meal times, when all the family were gathered about the table.

Floo—black-haired like Mitts's mother—would toddle up to Heinmein and tug at the tail of his lab coat.

The first few times this happened, Mitts found himself almost hypnotised by the sight.

He was brought into mind of a nature documentary: a young, naïve member of a pride of lions going up to the aged, half-crazed male lion and batting him with a paw.

There was no telling if Heinmein might snap.

If he might kick out.

Knock Floo onto her back.

Shuffle off out of the kitchen, scowling, his dinner clenched in his fists.

Back to his darkened cove.

But that wasn't what happened at all.

Mitts would never forget the first time Floo reached up and grabbed a fistful of Heinmein's lab coat.

He could still recall how every muscle in his body had seemed to seize tight.

And then Heinmein had glanced down and . . . *smiled*.

Oh, it wasn't any great wonder.

He showed no teeth.

And he certainly didn't make any more fuss.

But, still, it was the first time Mitts had *ever* seen Heinmein break free of that sincere—*severe*—expression.

When this event continued to happen—when it transformed into a routine—Mitts's mother made a habit of rising up from her seat. Walking alongside Floo. Doing her best to keep Floo away from Heinmein.

To Mitts's mind, if Heinmein had been truly troubled by these little interactions with Floo, then why didn't he wait an hour?

Wait until the kitchen was deserted?

He could've claimed his dinner in peace, then.

The only conclusion Mitts could draw was that Heinmein *enjoyed* it.

A couple of weeks later, Mitts's suspicions were confirmed.

As with every mealtime, Floo clambered down from her high stool, toddled across the kitchen floor, and tugged at the back of Heinmein's lab coat.

This time, however, it appeared that nobody, except Mitts, actually noticed this little scene playing out.

For some reason, that particular night, Mitts's parents were so occupied by their dinner that they didn't so much as look up to check on Floo.

But Mitts was checking on her.

At first, when Floo tugged on Heinmein's lab coat, he didn't react.

He kept his back to her.

He continued to serve himself dinner.

Just those gentle, almost soothing, *clunk-clunk* sounds as he spooned steaming rice onto his metal tray.

Finally, though, when he had apparently got through with serving himself dinner, he set his tray down on the kitchen surface, turned around to look at Floo, and then—and Mitts would never *ever* forget the sight—he crouched down and shovelled his hands beneath her armpits, lifting her up.

Clutching her to his chest.

When Mitts's parents noticed the sight, they were just as dumbstruck as Mitts.

He thought that, like him, they simply *couldn't believe* the sight.

Heinmein had shown them that he did indeed possess tenderness.

Human feeling.

Empathy.

From that moment forward, whenever Floo would see Heinmein skulking about the Compound, she would stop and point at him, pronouncing, *"Dok-uh!"* in a loud and proud voice.

Heinmein would pause in his sweeping, dragging gait. And he would wave to her, a wide smile pinning back his lips.

Despite all this, though, Mitts didn't trust Heinmein.

Not as far as he could throw him.

———

Mitts got himself showered quickly.

He brushed his teeth.

Toothpaste, soap, shaving cream, was all in seemingly limitless supply.

Boxes and boxes of it could be found in any given maintenance cupboard.

Once, when Mitts had been several shades of bored, he had sat down with a notepad and thought through just how many people, considering the supplies, and the space, the Restricted Area might be able to support. And for how long.

He had come up with fifty people, more or less.

And he estimated they would be able to survive for up to ten years.

So, considering that there were only *five* of them in the Restricted Area, he drew the conclusion that they could get by for another century.

If 'getting by' was all they had in mind.

Mitts dressed himself in one of the many hand-me-down shirts his father had passed to him. He liked to wear them with a plain white t-shirt underneath, and with the sleeves rolled up to just above his elbow. Then he would leave the first few buttons undone too.

His mother had done a good job adjusting some of his father's jeans. Before, when his father had first passed Mitts clothes for him to wear, he had walked about the Compound dragging the cuffs of the trousers all over the floors.

Mitts stepped into the kitchen and was, at once, over-whelmed by the sweet smell of something delicious cooking in one of the ovens.

Already, Mitts could taste the congealing, powdered eggs and butter, the rising flour, catching at the back of his throat.

All those smells, they reminded him of how things had been before.

Of happier times . . .

The air was warmed by the ovens. Mitts undid a couple more buttons of his shirt, so he further exposed the plain t-shirt he wore underneath.

His father and Floo were sat at the large kitchen table,

playing Snap with a well-thumbed deck of cards. Like always, Floo was wearing one of the dresses which their mother had sewn together from odds and ends. This one, Mitts could tell, had been salvaged from one—or *several*—pairs of jeans.

Though Mitts's mother's earlier efforts had seemed a little shabby, she had got better with practice.

Much better than his *father*, in any case.

His father hadn't changed his dress style in the seven years they'd been living in the Compound.

To be fair, though, there really hadn't been much opportunity for fashion experimentation—not for *any* of them.

That all might be changing soon, though.

If Mitts had his way.

If everything went to plan.

When Mitts glanced over to the oven, he saw his mother. A well-stained black apron was tied on tight about the front of her grey-blue, blouse.

Underneath, she wore a pair of well-adjusted jeans which —Mitts couldn't help noticing—bulged just a little at the seams.

Over the years, all of them had seemed to embrace the Compound.

They had all got a touch chubbier.

It wasn't like there was any exercise to be had, beyond running through the corridors.

And since it was so easy to get bored, they sometimes ate as entertainment.

Even Mitts seemed to have gained weight, though he tried to convert whatever fat stuck to him into muscle. He performed incessant press-ups, sit-ups, and those aforementioned runs through the corridors of the Restricted Area.

Mitts's mother looked back at him.

She coloured a touch—blushing.

"Oh," she said, and then turned around to look at Mitts's father and Floo. "We weren't expecting you to be up and about so early."

Mitts guessed his family had got so used to his teenage sleeping patterns—Mitts would often sleep in the 'daytime'—that they could plan around him.

Without him noticing.

What other top-secret operations might his family have planned without his knowledge?

Whatever they were—if they *did* exist at all—they surely couldn't be a patch on what *he* had planned . . .

Although Mitts understood, from the books he read, that parents had a habit of calling teenagers out for sleeping in all day, his parents never did.

He wondered if it might have something to do with his 'condition'.

With how he had seemingly 'got over' whatever ailment it was that he'd been suffering from.

Maybe they thought Mitts's lengthy sleeping patterns had to do with his miraculous recovery.

But Mitts didn't feel all that miraculous.

All that *special*.

Apart from the weird visions, the lucid dreams . . . that strange encounter he'd had seven years ago when he'd crawled through the air ducts, come face to face with that grey-purple hunk of flesh . . . he thought of himself as a reasonably normal kid.

Though what did 'reasonably normal' even mean?

As far as he knew, he might be the only eighteen-year-old kid on the planet.

Now, that was a scary thought . . .

Was there anything as scary as being unique?

Mitts took up his place at the kitchen table, realising in short order why his mother had blushed.

She was, of course, baking his birthday cake.

His mother turned her back on the oven and pressed on a guilty smile. "Well," she said, "it should only be ten minutes, I was hoping to have it on the table by the time you got out of bed."

Mitts glanced to his father and Floo.

In that moment, Floo, kneeling up on her high stool so that she could get the best view of the surface, turned over a card and then immediately, with a slap which shook the entire table top, cried, "SNAP!"

Mitts turned back to his mother, who was smiling again.

"But," she said, "I'd be surprised if *anyone* could sleep with *that* racket going on."

Mitts shrugged his shoulders. He had a few aches from the press-ups he'd done the night before.

Whenever he did any serious thinking, he worked out.

And he had had some *serious* thinking to do all right.

Maybe he'd overdone it a little.

He massaged his left upper arm, feeling a little knot just below the bicep.

"You're looking buff," his father put in.

Feeling a touch distracted, off in his own little world, as he found himself more and more these days, Mitts put on the best polite smile he could muster, and said, "Yeah, I don't want to turn into a blob, or anything."

His father laid a card down, and—as a result—Floo hammered down her palm on top of it, declaring, again, "SNAP!"

"It's one thing turning into a 'blob'," his father replied, "it's another to try and buff yourself up into some sort of superhero."

Mitts sniffed a laugh. He wondered if—perhaps—his father might've taken that as an underhanded jibe at his weight gain over these seven years.

But that was the truth.

Whereas before, his father had been just like him—skinny as a pole, not a scrap of extra fat on him—his father had grown consistently podgier as the years passed by.

So much so that he now wore the waistband of his jeans slung beneath his burgeoning gut.

Mitts's mother, over at the oven, announced that the cake was ready for serving.

And then she made the same non-joke she had made every single birthday since they had resided in the Compound. The one about them having to *imagine* candles because they had none.

But Mitts was done with imagining.

He was done with the Compound.

With the Restricted Area.

Now was the time to move on.

To get back out into the real world.

As Mitts's mother laid the cake before him, as his family all sang him happy birthday, Mitts found his gaze wandering. Over to the kitchen doorway.

He saw him there.

Heinmein.

Lurking.

Just like the early days, Heinmein refused to use crutches. But, for some reason, when Mitts had observed Heinmein out in the corridors, he noted that he no longer had the same difficulties walking.

In fact, when Mitts did observe him walking about the corridors of the Restricted Area, he noticed that Heinmein now had a fairly normal gait.

His cleanliness, too, had improved.

Mitts didn't feel anywhere near as hostile toward him as he had in the early days.

For whatever purpose, Heinmein *had* attempted to cure him.

And whether Heinmein had fed him some sort of unintended miracle cure, or if there had been some other factor in play, Mitts had to give Heinmein some credit for at least *attempting* to save his life.

And, to tell the truth, that knowledge *rankled* him.

How was Mitts *ever* supposed to repay a gesture like that?

When the singing reached its climax, and then gave way to clapping, Mitts realised he was still staring at the doorway.

Still staring at Heinmein.

And that Heinmein was clapping along.

Mitts turned back to his birthday cake.

As he cut the cake, he thought about how Heinmein was the only one who could *possibly* have an inkling of what he had planned.

Heinmein was the only one who could possibly stop him.

———

Mitts waited until the fluorescent strip lights had faded down in their imitation of night. He flipped on his torch as he always did. He shone its yellowish circle of light into the gloom.

Normally, he would lie propped up in bed reading into the early hours. Seeing as he had worked his way through all the novels his family had brought into the Compound in the first place, he had started to make a habit of digging into a small room toward the edge of the Restricted Area.

One which had a series of manuals; technical handbooks.

At first, when Mitts had set foot across the threshold of that room, breathed in the slightly acrid smell of glue from book bindings, felt the cool tingle of the air conditioning up against his skin, it had been like he was trespassing.

For some reason—*sometimes*—he felt his mind swimming back to those earlier fears.

Back when he had thought that at any second a group of heavily armed security personnel might come busting in through the blast doors.

Bringing them all down in a rain of semi-automatic rifle fire.

Actually, when Mitts had thought about his feelings in crossing over into that room in more detail, he realised that he had believed it to be a part of the Restricted Area kept under close guard by Heinmein.

He supposed that Heinmein frequently visited the room, for tips on whatever problem he might have been facing that particular day.

Having said that, though, Mitts had never actually come upon Heinmein on his frequent visits to the impromptu library.

And neither had Heinmein said anything to Mitts about his visits here.

So Mitts thought himself in the clear.

Over the time he had resided in the Compound, he had gone through manuals detailing electrical engineering, basic plumbing and other skills which he never would've been capable of learning off his father.

Back home—back in *another* life—his father had been an accountant.

There wasn't much use for accountants now.

Once Mitts had grappled with those skills, he turned his attention to the books on physics, chemistry, biology; all of those subjects which'd bored him to death at school, but which now, in the Compound, with no other stimuli, seemed fascinating.

One of the books had even contained a map of the Compound itself.

He had torn out the page and shoved it into his jeans pocket.

Mitts grasped the rubber grip of his torch tightly, feeling the texture of the rubber squeeze against his skin. He shone the light over the latest book he had been leafing through:

A Practical Introduction to Machine Coding

It was one of the last books in the library.

It'd only taken him seven years to get through a thousand, or so, books.

For the past couple of years, Mitts had been reading up on computer skills. Learning all the basics. Several times, he had stolen into those emptied rooms which contained dozens of computers. And although all of them had been dead—there was no power allocated to those rooms, and the computers' circuitry had been long ago fried—he would practise the lines of code in the books, his fingers flurrying over the keypad as he copied the written commands.

Committing them to memory.

The way Mitts liked to think of it, computer program-ming—for him—was sort of like constantly completing a three-dimensional puzzle within his own mind.

And it was a *perfect* means of removing his focus from the present.

From the Compound.

From the Restricted Area.

Mitts turned the circle of light onto his camp bed. Onto his sports bag—the same one he had arrived here with all those years ago.

The one which, back in school, he had used to store his PE kit.

He shovelled up the three or four books on computers into the bag. He laid them on top of the clothes he had already bundled in there.

Only when he looked around the room—what had served as his bedroom for the past seven years—did he realise that he had nothing else left to pack.

That everything which was his *in the world* was now nestled within that sad, little, plump sports bag.

Mitts breathed in.

Then out.

It might be the last time—for a long time—that he got to breathe the air like a normal human being.

He glanced down to his bedside table, to where he had left the folded-up note.

He turned away from it quickly. He didn't want to dwell on the contents of his scrawled handwriting within.

He needed to have his mind straight.

His plan depended on him being able to think straight.

On him not getting carried away.

Decided, he glanced upward.

To the ventilation hatch.

And then he went to work with the screwdriver.

———

Following the map he pictured in his mind, the supplementary section of one of those books about the Compound, Mitts dragged himself through the air vents. He counted the openings as he went, dropping down through the third one on his left.

He wasn't subtle about opening the ventilation hatch.

He tucked his knee back into his chest and then kicked out.

The hatch busted open.

It clattered down into the room below.

Each year he'd done it, getting through the air vents had

been a successively more difficult squeeze for Mitts. And today, he had found it the toughest so far.

That had been another factor in his decision.

What might happen when he was too large to fit through the air vents at all?

Then the only way out of the Restricted Area would be through the blast doors. Although Mitts knew that he simply *had* to get out, he wasn't prepared to put his family at risk while doing so.

If he died right now—if he got poisoned—then he would be the only one harmed.

For some reason, he didn't think that was going to happen.

He liked to believe—because of his sickness; because he'd almost died—that he was stronger than the others.

Better able to resist.

At least these night-time visits outside of the Restricted Area, into the wider Compound, didn't seem to have left any lasting damage on him.

Nothing Heinmein, in seven years of weekly check-ups, had observed, in any case.

Mitts shone his torch around.

It was a windowless room, just as it had been marked on the plan.

He had peered in here before, but hadn't yet visited . . . thus why he'd had to bust through the ventilation hatch.

The room consisted of a simple wooden bench down the

middle, much like the changing rooms which Mitts had been forced to use back at school, for PE.

Instead of there being lockers placed all around, and a slight scent of soap lather and mud from the showers, the air stank strongly of disinfectant.

He wondered if *that* had been the odour he'd smelled all that time ago.

The motivating factor for him wanting to explore the ventilation hatch.

He studied the room.

He noted the showerhead-like devices which hung down from the ceiling.

He supposed that was where the disinfectant came from.

A spray.

He guessed the spray system was running off some kind of backup unit. There was no other explanation for it to still be functioning after all these years.

In all his explorations of the Compound at night, he had never come across another soul.

Not even bodies.

The whole Compound was deserted.

At least as far as he could make out.

Mitts observed the white, semi-transparent overalls which hung down off the hooks which surrounded the room. He trod along, looking to the eerie masks which accompanied them.

They had those chrome, gasmask mouthpieces.

The ones Mitts had seen in a few films.

The ones he had seen in diagram form in several of the manuals he'd read through.

Mitts removed one of the suits off its peg. As he brought it close to him, the smell of disinfectant was almost unbearable. He had a strong urge to simply drop the suit.

To allow it to slide through his fingers.

But he held on.

Within his own mind, Mitts went through the steps of using the suit.

First, there was the zip.

He undid it all the way.

And then he located the little computer panel around the back of the suit.

This was the part he was most unsure of.

He tapped the Power button.

A green energy bar blinked on.

Full.

Mitts stood, his face illuminated by the bright-green display.

He looked about the other suits in the room.

He wondered if they were all charged up too.

He tried out the few suits nearest to him.

All had their energy bars at full.

Working quickly, he snaffled the battery packs off the suits. He slotted them into his sports bag which hung down off his shoulder. He made sure to take all of them that he could.

With the combined battery power, he hoped to survive for months outside the Compound.

That done, Mitts stuffed a couple of the suits into his sports bag, seeing as they didn't occupy too much space. If he snagged a hole in the suit he was wearing, it would be simpler to ditch it and put on a fresh one than to try and mend the damage.

He set about getting into the suit he had chosen.

He zipped it all the way up, held the helmet beneath his arm and then headed for the door.

The security keypad had power.

And the electromagnetic lock was engaged.

That was unexpected.

But it wasn't an obstacle.

Digging into the knowledge he'd accumulated through all the manuals he'd read, Mitts used the manual-override code on the keypad.

The locks snicked back.

And Mitts plodded through the door.

Mitts had spent so many night-time hours prowling about the Compound that he was almost on autopilot as he swooped through the corridors.

He didn't pause for any kind of a nostalgic moment. He felt nothing for the Compound. All the same, he would've thought that, after seven years here, he would feel *something*.

Somehow, he just couldn't accept the Compound had been his home.

Or as close to a 'home' as it was possible to get.

Mitts made his way into the reception area of the Compound, where he put on the helmet. As he recalled it from the manuals he had leafed through, there had been a further three security points for anybody entering from the outside wishing to get here.

But there was no power in these outer areas.

Mitts had simply to push the rusted-up exterior door open.

He barged it with his shoulder, glad for all those sit-ups and press-ups.

They'd given him strength.

Before Mitts could really work out what he had done, he realised that he was out into the night-time air.

His surprise was so great that he almost forgot to flip the switch at the back of his suit.

The one which would allow him to breathe.

———

Breathing in the air of the suit was like sucking on disinfectant, straight from a plastic bottle.

Mitts felt it dry out his mouth. At the same time, it brought all the saliva in his tongue to the surface. He could hear the gentle, rhythmic *tick-tick* as the breathing apparatus responded to his respiration.

Already, he felt hot in the suit.

Mitts followed the exterior fence which ran around the Compound. At one point, he reached a gate. He unzipped his sports bag and produced a pair of wire cutters. He snipped a nice, big hole.

Then he ducked down and stepped through.

On the other side, Mitts glanced back over his shoulder.

A series of squat, cement buildings, lit up in the moonlight.

The Compound.

An ugly place.

Mitts's focus drifted up to the moon.

He stood staring at it for a long while.

Often, Mitts would leave his bedroom behind, sneak out through the air vents just so that he might slump himself up by an exterior hatch and stare at the moon.

It made him feel almost as if he was back home again.

Almost as if things were back to normal.

Once, Mitts had stayed out in the air vent for the whole night, waiting for the sun to rise up on the horizon. But he didn't seem to be able to pick out a vantage point where he could look at it directly.

All he could make out from his position in the air vent were the secondary details: the sun rays licking the concrete surrounding the Compound.

Mitts fixed his mind on his destination, guiding himself about the wire fence.

He used the Compound's scattered buildings as a guide for his progress.

There was that one run of buildings which, at least on the plans, looked like it might form the shape of a top hat. He ran his eyes over the Compound, searching for that feature.

He found it.

Made toward it.

He took care not to break into anything more than a fast walk.

He didn't want to trip and fall.

There was no telling what damage he might do.

A broken leg wouldn't be any way to start off the journey.

He made his way around the back of the top hat-looking section of building, and then he went on a little further, past the pineapple-shaped outbuilding.

Then he turned his focus to searching.

He looked over the Compound.

Looking for it.

It *had* to be here.

Mitts glanced up and—finally—he saw it.

The ventilation hatch which, for the first time, seven years ago, Mitts had sat slumped up against. The vantage point from which he had looked out on the outside world.

But that was only *part* of what Mitts was looking for.

He turned his gaze downward. To the wall beneath the ventilation hatch.

And he saw . . . nothing.

What had he expected?

It *had* been seven years.

There was nothing there.

Still, he couldn't help but pace over.

He cut through the once-electrified wire fence.

Let himself through to the other side.

He stared down at the cement, looking for some sort of clue.

Something that might just give him a *hint*.

When Mitts squinted, he thought he might be able to see a damp patch on the concrete. But, the more he brought his vision clear—*sharper*—he became more and more convinced that he was only fooling himself.

'Bringing the wool down over his eyes'.

He had read that expression in one of the many novels his parents had brought along into the Restricted Area.

Mitts felt his gut sink slightly. He had hoped that he might find something to either confirm, or deny, what he had seen seven years ago.

But, no . . .

Everything was just as muddy as it had been before.

Mitts moved on.

He knew—*logically speaking*—he needed to cover as

much ground as he possibly could during the night, before the sun came up.

Because, when the sun *did* come up, Mitts would have no idea what to expect.

He turned away from the scene which'd so haunted him all these seven years—had haunted him so much that he hadn't returned to this spot where he had seen that . . . that *creature.*

Not until tonight.

Mitts headed back toward the wire fence. Away once again from the place he had lived these past years. He did feel a slight sinking disappointment.

He would've liked to have found *something.*

Anything at all.

He set off back across the Compound.

Made it to the fence.

And then, from out of the darkness, there came a bright —*overpoweringly bright*—light.

It shone all over him.

Froze him.

He turned around.

Held his suited forearm up to the visor of his suit.

He heard his breathing coming faster now.

The staccato *tick-tick-tick-tick-tick* from his suit as his breathing pulled hard on the oxygen tanks.

Several beads of sweat rolled down his face.

A salty smell.

The *taste* of salt on his lips.

A spotlight, that was what it was.

He recalled from the plans.

But he couldn't recall anything about automation.

Though that didn't mean there *wasn't* any automation.

Was this another section of the Compound which continued to have power?

Now that his eyes had adjusted a little to the bright light, he realised that there was a silhouette standing by the side of the machine. He tracked the silhouette.

He would've known that silhouette anywhere.

Just about *anywhere.*

He knew that silhouette now.

Heinmein.

———

Mitts thought about running. About escaping.

But something rooted him to the spot.

He couldn't leave.

He couldn't leave *now.*

Danger . . . he felt it in the air.

Before he could make any sort of conscious decision, he was striding back toward the Compound.

Headed for the reception area.

Back in the building, Mitts was confronted by Heinmein.

As always, he was dressed in his tatty lab coat.

Heinmein's eyes were wide. His pupils inflamed by the lenses of his thick glasses. "You found your way out?" he said.

Before Mitts could say anything at all, Heinmein added, "But how . . . how did you manage it?"

Mitts told him about the air vents.

That he had come up here often, at night.

He said nothing about the grey-purple skinned being he had encountered those seven years earlier.

Heinmein's glare never left him throughout the whole of the story.

Mitts waited uneasily for Heinmein to break out of his daze.

Surely he was fixing to attack.

However, Heinmein only reached up to adjust the lie of his glasses across the bridge of his nose.

He nodded to the suit which Mitts wore. "And I see that you found some toys?"

Mitts felt himself blush a little, though he didn't quite realise why.

After all, he had made up his mind and he was determined to stick with his choice.

For him, there was no returning to the Restricted Area, and Heinmein might as well know *why*.

"I'm sick of it," Mitts said, staring right into Heinmein's black eyes, "sick of how you treat us all as living experiments."

Heinmein remained still.

"I know you keep records—are using us for your research, for whatever end it might be." Mitts shook his head. "I don't want to be part of it anymore."

Heinmein didn't reply right away, and Mitts saw him swallow hard, watched his Adam's apple bobble in his throat. And then he responded, "What about your family? You are not concerned about them?"

Mitts felt his chest tighten. Although he had thought over his response about a million times in his own head, it was totally different now that he had to say the words out loud.

Almost as it, every time he opened his mouth, his throat closed up on him.

In the end, Mitts could only squeeze out a single syllable, "No."

Heinmein continued to stare hard at him. His gaze was unflinching, as if he was merely looking at a test specimen . . . and what else was Mitts to Heinmein?

"How long?" Mitts said. "How long have you been coming up here—how long has it been safe to leave the Restricted Area?"

Heinmein flashed his eyes, gave a slight sigh. "Well—*safe* —that really is a relative term, is it not?" He glanced beyond Mitts, in such a way that Mitts was almost convinced there might be someone standing behind him.

It took all his resolve *not* to turn and look.

Mitts wondered, haphazardly, if Heinmein might be armed.

He had come across several rooms on the Compound with assorted weapons.

But he had always left them well alone.

Could he really trust Heinmein would've done the same?

Heinmein nodded to Mitts, and then to his sports bag. "You have seen for yourself that I keep the power up and running for those battery packs, and that it is my custom to use one of those suits if up in the Compound for any sustained period of time." He cocked his head to one side. "And if I go *outside*, why, then it is a necessity."

Mitts tightened his hold on the strap of his sports bag.

It was time to go.

"So," Mitts said, "are you planning to stop me?"

Heinmein remained straight faced for several moments.

And then his expression cracked.

His mouth widened into a jagged-toothed smile.

"Of course not," Heinmein said, spreading his hands wide, "that was not what I had planned at all." He paused for a moment, and then added, "But there was something which I believe you might have an interest in seeing."

"What?" Mitts fired back.

Heinmein gave a nonchalant shrug of his shoulders, still smiling that grimy smile. "The reason *why* you are still alive."

———

Mitts made no move to leave his sports bag behind in the

reception area, neither did he make any gesture to take off his suit. And Heinmein said nothing about Mitts's decision to walk through the corridors of the Compound still dressed as he was.

Heinmein led him down a series of staircases, onto what Mitts calculated to be the third basement level. It was an area of the Compound that Mitts had never got around to studying.

Most likely because, when he'd looked at the plan, there had been nothing that'd immediately attracted his attention.

No store cupboards of particular interest.

Heinmein brought Mitts past a series of metal doors, each with etched metal plaques fastened to them. All of the plaques had long-winded names which Mitts never had the chance to take in fully.

When they reached the end of the corridor, though, and Heinmein produced a jingling keyring from within one of the pockets of his lab coat, Mitts made out what the plaque said:

Autopsy

Mitts slipped Heinmein a sidelong glance. "What was this place used for?"

Already focused on slipping the key into the lock, Heinmein gave a side-on shrug and mumbled, "Governmental purposes."

As Mitts heard the key *snick* in the lock, he found himself reaching out, grabbing hold of Heinmein's forearm. He felt how frail Heinmein's bones felt, how layers of fat hung off his arm, and when he looked once more into the doctor's black eyes, he saw that he was frightened.

Frightened of him?

"What did *you* do here?"

Heinmein's eyes widened a touch more.

Then he looked away. "I did certain things with bio-chemical body modifications . . ."

Mitts tightened his grip. "What does that mean?"

Heinmein, trembling now, looked back, then said, "I conducted experiments on *humans*—on *soldiers*—certain projects that were designed to help the *Army*."

"The 'Army'? " Mitts replied, finally releasing Hein-mein's arm.

"Yes," Heinmein said, turning the key in the lock, and then pushing the door open. He outstretched his arm, and tilted his head to one side in a deferential, almost sarcastic, way. "Please," he said, "after you."

Mitts stepped in over the threshold and found himself, almost right away, overpowered by the glimmering metal in the bright light. He looked about him, to the wall.

A series of gigantic filing cabinets.

Each one with a tag assigned to it:

Alpha-numeric sequences that meant nothing at all to him.

But he supposed they meant an awful lot indeed to some shutdown database.

In the middle of the room, there was a stainless-steel table

—much like the one which Mitts had become accustomed to back in the Restricted Area.

Mitts glanced to Heinmein, looking for some sort of clue as to what was expected of him.

Heinmein dipped his head, and padded off toward the enormous filing cabinet which filled the entirety of the wall. Then, scooting along to one of the drawers he had, apparently, already marked out in his mind, he fished another key from his keyring and turned it in the lock.

What Mitts saw next, he couldn't quite believe.

Heinmein brought the drawer sliding out with an unbearable *screech* of hinges.

On the drawer Mitts observed the bagged-up form.

An overpowering stench of sulphur entered the air.

Spiked the air.

Heinmein glanced back at Mitts. He batted his left eyelid. Nothing more than a nervous twitch; but a *nervous* twitch all the same.

He reached out and took hold of the zipper on the bag, and then, with Mitts moving closer still, to get a good look over Heinmein's shoulder, he pulled it open.

Mitts looked down.

On the grey-purple flesh.

On the body which, at first, seemed to have no form.

Mitts felt his mind melting within his skull.

His heart rose up to his throat.

It beat hard against his skin.

He reached up to touch his pulse, to check that he wasn't imagining this.

That this wasn't another one of his lucid dreams.

"Is it . . ." Mitts got out.

Without turning to look at him, Heinmein gave a nod. He spoke his next few words through a sigh, "Dead, yes, when I found it." He paused for several seconds and then added, "Outside the Compound."

Mitts felt a dizzy spell catch him.

He breathed in deeply.

Tried to calm himself down.

But he could hardly keep himself still.

He felt his leg jigging, uncontrollably.

Energy bouncing through him.

Mitts tried to clear his vision. To bring his mind back to just what was going on here. That what he had seen—seven years ago—had in fact been real. He stared down at the body once more, this time hoping that he would better understand.

He started at the head.

An inflated mass of grey-purple flesh.

Then he moved downward.

To the neck.

The creature's skin reminded Mitts of whale blubber, of what he'd seen of whales in nature documentaries. He wondered if the flesh was still wet to the touch.

Mitts thought about reaching out.

Thought about *touching* the skin.

But he held back.

Something told him that he and Heinmein might be in great danger here.

When Mitts reached the mid-section of the creature, he saw what resembled a stomach. It was bulbous, sticking out . . . it reminded Mitts of pictures he had seen in textbooks:

Round-stomached patients suffering from liver diseases.

There was a series of sewn-up scars down the creatures stomach, and this was where, Mitts imagined, Heinmein had conducted the autopsy; where he had attempted to bring the creature's secrets out into the harsh, bright light of the room.

The creature had two arms, too, just like them.

But no feet.

As if he had read Mitts's mind, Heinmein said, "Although I never saw it alive, I believe it would move by dragging its body across the ground."

Mitts felt his chest tighten again. He thought back to that day. To the day when he had slumped himself up there, against the ventilation hatch.

Heinmein continued to gaze down on the creature as if this might be the very first time he had actually inspected it. Then he glanced back at Mitts. "You saw this before, didn't you?"

Mitts had no idea what to say.

The question was so direct.

There seemed no way to dodge it.

". . . Yes," Mitts managed to get out, his mouth feeling

impossibly dry and a stale taste smothering his tongue.

Heinmein went on, like a policeman reeling through his interpretation of events, stopping only briefly to have a witness confirm or deny his deductions, "I found this creature by one of the exterior air vents. It was dead when I reached it." He turned to look at Mitts, with his black eyes. "You saw it alive, did you not?"

Again, there seemed no room for Mitts to deny the fact. "Yes," he said.

Heinmein gave a nod, then turned his attention back down to the creature. "When I discovered the cadaver, out there, below the ventilation hatch, I looked around for more of them—it seemed to me that there *should* have been more of them." He inspected Mitts very closely. "Did *you* see any more of them?"

"No," Mitts replied, turning back to look at the creature.

Heinmein breathed in deeply and then sighed back out. He rested his fingers on the edge of the drawer, as if making to slide it back inside the giant filing cabinet.

But he hesitated.

He didn't slide it back just yet.

"You noticed a change, didn't you?" Heinmein said. "I mean, after you had the encounter with this creature—that was the reason why you got better, no?"

Mitts held himself still for a long while.

There was something just so surreal about this whole conversation.

He couldn't quite get his head around it.

Although he had believed, all along, that his encounter with the creature had led to his miraculous recovery, within his own mind Mitts had promised himself that he would never share this inkling with anyone else.

But Heinmein had seen through him so easily.

Finally, Mitts replied, "Yes . . . 'a change' . . . and"—Mitts thought about it for a moment, and then decided there was no reason to leave any information out—"visions, strange dreams, these . . . just these *hills* . . . these dark-purple hills."

When Mitts glanced back at Heinmein, he was surprised to see his mouth latched open.

As if he was in shock.

"Did you see them too?" Mitts asked.

Heinmein, clearly stunned, shook his head. "No, I have seen nothing of that."

Mitts turned back to the creature, lying on the drawer.

He could feel Heinmein's scrutinising gaze.

Like a heat lamp.

"All my life I have had trouble with walking"—Heinmein slapped his affected leg—"but soon after I brought this creature in here, as soon as I began the procedures, trying to determine what it was, where it came from, I too noticed a change in me."

Heinmein stepped away from the opened drawer which bore the body of the creature. "Do you not believe that I have a—how should I say?—rather *youthful* look about me now?"

Mitts had to admit that he had noticed a change.

Heinmein was shaking his head, as if out of disbelief. "Never in my *life* would I have believed it unless I had seen it for myself." He nodded to Mitts. "And you—you must feel somewhat similar, no? This is like a realm of magic, and mystery, something which could not exist—which *should* not exist."

Mitts, though, felt his mind shifting gears.

Turning its attention to more practical matters.

"What does it mean?" Mitts asked. "Where did this come from?"

Heinmein continued to shake his head.

His smile became so wide that apprehension gripped him.

Mitts glanced down.

Saw that Heinmein, from somewhere—*somehow*—had grabbed hold of a gun.

He held it pointed at him.

Mitts glanced back up.

Took in the maniacal look in Heinmein's eye.

The arched eyebrows.

He had waited so long for his human specimen.

Now he had his chance.

"Stop!" Mitts called out.

But it was too late.

Out of darkness, a bullet bit him.

Sam America could feel the winds gathering up their skirts, preparing to loop their arms and trot all the way down along the coast.

Pummelling all in their path.

Leaving nothing but desolation.

Despair.

Testing fortitude.

While he walked, he kicked at the stones. Sent them skittering down toward the tide—the tide which continued to slosh in; a long-suffering, terminal patient drawing its last breaths; only able to breathe with the aid of a ventilator.

The stony shore was a foreboding place for Sam America . . . for the last hero on the face of Planet Earth.

But he held himself still—he held himself tall—and, within his mind, he heard the constant reminder of just what he fought for.

Of all there was to gain.

Because mankind—the world—wasn't a lost cause.

Not yet.

Not quite yet.

THE HUMAN SPECIMEN

Mitts *came to his senses*, struggling to reach the battery-powered pack at the back of his suit.

He was trembling.

All over.

He was losing blood quickly.

He could feel blood dampening his suit.

Trickling down his spine.

Down the backs of his legs.

The coppery smell of blood—*its bitter taste*—filled his airways.

His mind had got away from him.

It was almost as if it'd been a dream.

Or as if, for the past few minutes—had they been hours? —his brain and body had become divided.

His mind operating on another plane . . . that superhero

figure again; that *Sam America* . . . while his body . . . his body had . . .

Finally, Mitts managed to reach the battery-powered pack.

He flipped the switch.

Tick. Tick. Tick, went the mechanism.

He could breathe again.

He marched on his way, out of the Compound, across the cement.

Clutching his side, his breaths came hard and shallow.

As Mitts stumbled through the hole he had cut in the wire fence, he was dimly aware that the sun was out. And that its rays streamed down. He felt them warm the space between his shoulders.

Gently—*ever so gently*—cooking him alive.

Every step, he was losing energy.

He was certain that, sometime soon, he would lose the ability to put one foot before the other.

But he found the drive to keep going.

To keep himself going.

He *had* to.

As Mitts had lain on the floor of the Autopsy room, he had felt the pain shuddering through him.

He had felt the hot, sharp sensation digging into his side.

From the bullet.

And yet, he had still felt that strength—the same strength

which had been visited upon him when he'd first come across the creature—when it had been alive.

Mitts had known that he would only get one chance.

And that he couldn't make a mistake.

As Heinmein had stood above him, he had explained how he had murdered every member of Mitts's family.

How, when Heinmein had noticed Mitts had gone missing, he had put the gun to each one of their heads and —*simply*—blown them away.

They had all been dead by the time Heinmein had shone the spotlight.

At that moment, Mitts had felt his fingers forming fists, quite aside from his inner will.

It was a wonder that he hadn't launched himself onto his feet.

Had a go at pummelling Heinmein with his fists.

Right there and then.

But he had found a larger inner strength.

Patience.

To play the waiting game.

Mitts had waited for Heinmein to draw close, and then, with a single rush of blood through his veins, he had kicked out, caught the back of Heinmein's leg, sent him plunging backward, the gun firing off a shot into the roof of the Autopsy room.

Mitts recalled how he had winced when the back of

Heinmein's head struck the drawer which contained the specimen.

For a long few seconds, Mitts had felt his pulse pumping hard, working to accompany the pain he felt pounding away in his side as blood eked out of him.

Mitts thought about Heinmein's face, about how he had lain on his back, his mouth opened in an eternal yawn.

The worst part of it—the *very* worst part of it—was that Mitts had been right all along.

About Heinmein.

About *not* trusting him.

But none of his family had seemed to feel the same danger, none of them seemed to have slotted the pieces together as Mitts had.

Realised that the reason their neighbour, Heinmein, the strange old loner across the road, had chosen them over all the others on their street, was because they were a family.

Because he had known, somehow, that Mitts's mother had been pregnant.

Because he had known he could perform his experiments.

In peace.

Mitts thought about how Heinmein must've had some sort of advance-warning system set up throughout the Compound. He had known that Mitts had slipped out of the Restricted Area, and that he was planning to leave.

Mitts supposed he hadn't been subtle in his escape efforts after all.

And when Heinmein had caught wind of Mitts's fledgling escape, he had panicked, decided there was no reason for keeping Mitts's family alive any longer.

Not if Mitts himself was planning to abscond.

Only now, as Mitts felt his trainers crunch on the dirt outside the fence of the Compound, did he realise that he had been Heinmein's experiment all along—all through these seven years.

Despite his father's well-intentioned demands that Heinmein leave Mitts alone, Heinmein had merely been biding his time.

Waiting.

With Mitts alone, in the Autopsy room, his family already dead, Heinmein had clearly panicked.

He had had no idea what to do now that his pet science project was so determined to leave.

To escape him.

Once Mitts had checked on Heinmein's pulse, felt that skittering sense of loathing tingle all over the surface of his skin, he had opened the blast doors to the Restricted Area.

He had checked every one of the neat bullet holes in each one of his family's foreheads.

Just as Heinmein would've wished it.

Clean, clinical.

Concluded.

On his way back out of the Compound, Mitts had found some medical supplies.

From one of the first-aid zones.

He had done his very best to disinfect the wound, to patch himself up with gauze and cotton wool.

As far as Mitts had been able to tell, the bullet hadn't lodged itself in his side.

But, among all those text books, there had only been basic first-aid care guides.

Certainly nothing to do with the surgery a bullet wound would—*surely*—require.

Mitts plodded on.

He could feel a few tears coming now.

Each one of them welling up in the corners of his eyes, hanging there for seconds before rolling down his face. He wished he could go back. He wished that he hadn't left at all.

It might all have been different if he hadn't become so decided, made it such a definite, unshiftable decision that he would leave.

He could've played along, continued with his routine within the Restricted Area.

His family surrounding him.

None the wiser.

And Heinmein would've been placated.

Happy to wait—*perhaps forever*—for his human specimen.

But Mitts knew the truth, that, sooner or later, Heinmein would've tired.

And, as was clear from his desperate action in the

Autopsy room, Heinmein had no real question of conscience about whether he got his specimen dead or alive.

As the sun continued to beat down, the sports bag which Mitts lugged over his shoulder became almost like a lead weight. He had the urge to simply cast it off—to chuck it into the dirt which surrounded him.

But he told himself that he needed the supplies nestled within.

That if he didn't have the batteries for his suit then his life-support systems would soon run out.

Mitts slugged on for another few steps before he realised that—*really*—he couldn't care less whether he lived or died.

Because, if he did live, he would have to experience those images: the images of his dead family, staring back at him every single day.

Every time he closed his eyes.

Until he died . . .

Why postpone time?

What was the point?

There was no world left any longer.

Feeling the sweat pour down his face, and the pain in his side become almost too much to bear, Mitts swung back his arm, getting up momentum, and then he thrust forward, hurling the sports bag off into the air.

Sending it tumbling.

It landed with a puff of dust.

And Mitts dropped to his knees.

He lost himself to the heat.

And unconsciousness.

———

When Mitts awoke he could hear voices.

Distant voices.

Voices through walls.

For a second—for a *hopeful* second—he thought he had dreamed it all. That the nightmare hadn't played out in reality.

Before he opened his eyes, Mitts felt a smile find its way onto his face.

Sometimes his dreams were so real—so *lucid*—that he couldn't quite manage to convince himself that *dreams* were all they were.

Mitts opened his eyes.

His vision was bleary.

He could smell . . . *bacon?* . . . it had been so long since he had smelled bacon.

In the Compound—in the Restricted Area—there had been no meat, for obvious reasons. Only powdered substances. Tin cans of vegetables, pulses.

Mitts felt his stomach quiver out of anticipation.

He wondered if his mother had managed to dig up some bacon from *somewhere* . . . or, perhaps, as Mitts had often fantasised, someone had come to save them.

Maybe it was a group of soldiers, with fresh supplies for survivors.

Could it be that they weren't all alone in the world after all?

Mitts blinked several times, trying to bring the world clear.

He was lying on his side.

On a bed . . . *not* his camp bed back in the Restricted Area.

His stomach dipped.

First of all, he brought the foreground into focus.

Bars.

Grey, steel bars.

Mitts stared at them. Unable to believe it.

But then he told himself he must.

A cell.

A jail cell.

He peered through the gaps in the bars.

A small, confined corridor.

Concrete walls.

A heavy-looking steel door at the other end.

There was a tiny, letterbox-sized window high up on the wall.

He caught several golden rays of sunlight—*sunset?*—glimmering through the gap.

For Mitts, it was almost blinding.

He held his forearm up to shield his eyes, and felt the

burn at the back of his eye sockets. His brain felt as if it was retreating into the recesses of his skull.

He glanced about himself.

Over his prostrate body.

He traced the outline of his body beneath the frayed, brown blanket which was draped over him.

He glanced down, to the floor, to the *stone* floor.

His trainers had been neatly placed there. One pushed up against the other.

A sock stuffed into each.

He glanced about for his sports bag, but couldn't see it anywhere.

Then he remembered he had tossed it.

He had thrown it away as he had fallen to his knees.

He breathed in deeply, trying to stir something within his body, to bring on some sort of recollection.

So, his dream had been real.

It had all happened.

But, if so, then where was he right now?

All he could remember was giving up—*having given up*—and how he had lain down in the warm dirt, and just drifted off with the . . . with the . . .

He reached for his side, where he had been shot.

He realised that though he had been stripped of his over-alls, and of the shirt he had worn beneath, he still had on the plain, white t-shirt, and his jeans.

When he danced his fingertips across the wound, he felt a severe pain.

He stop touching it.

Feeling pain throb through him, he took extreme care to peel back his blanket.

He tilted his head and looked down at his midriff.

His plain white t-shirt had turned a brown-red shade.

When Mitts touched the material, it felt crusty.

Hands trembling, worried that he might send blinding pain skittering through his body, he reached down for the hem of his t-shirt.

Working carefully, he prised his fingertips beneath the material.

Ever so slowly, he peeled it back.

Mitts held his breath as he worked, as he gently unrolled the t-shirt from his stomach.

As he brought his t-shirt up further and further he caught sight of a virginal, white bandage.

One which'd been strapped about his wound.

He stared at it, wondering how it had ended up there.

Who had dressed his wounds?

There wasn't so much as a speck of blood on the bandage itself, though his t-shirt was sodden with dried blood.

At the periphery of his hearing, he heard the *creak* of hinges.

The gentle tread of booted feet.

Mitts rolled his t-shirt back down over the bandage, but

not before he heard a snide voice saying, "Not a bad job even if I do say so myself."

Mitts turned his head to look.

A girl.

About his age.

Maybe a couple of years older.

Blond.

Blue-eyed.

Thin . . . her throat sharp as a razor's edge.

She wore a dark-green, sleeveless tank top which was tight against her compact breasts and abdomen.

Underneath she wore a pair of black jeans which, Mitts saw, had had the kneecaps slashed off.

She pursed her lips, causing the skin around her mouth to wrinkle.

Mitts couldn't help noticing the trio of scars which ran—almost like a three-fingered claw—down her left cheek.

" 'Bout time you got up, don't you think?" she said.

Mitts's gaze drifted and he saw, now, standing at her elbow there was an enormous guy—he had to be at least thirty, and he was probably twice, if not *three times*, Mitts's weight.

All muscle.

Like the blond girl, the muscled man wore a dark-green sleeveless tank top and black jeans.

He clutched a handgun, down at his thigh.

Although Mitts knew next to nothing about guns, he

could tell, from the look of the handgun's beaten-up casing, that it'd been through an awful lot.

Had a lot of use.

"Hey? Up here, numbnuts."

Mitts turned his attention away from the muscled man.

Back to the blond girl.

The girl was still smiling wryly. She paced up to the bars of Mitts's cell and then nodded in the direction of his midriff. "How you doing?"

Still stunned about where he was—and with about a million questions on his mind—he tried to haul himself up into a sitting position.

It was a difficult task.

When he propped himself up on his elbows, he felt a pang of pain flash through his side.

It sent a tingle down his spine.

He winced.

The man and girl laughed.

"Yeah," the girl said, "haven't we *all* been there before?"

Mitts looked to the muscled man with the handgun. He continued to hold it down at his thigh, pointing it at the floor. He thought about Heinmein's gun.

He scolded himself for not having thought to bring it with him.

But, most likely, he would've had the gun taken off him when he'd been found.

Realising he couldn't so much as move a muscle without giving himself more pain, he decided it better to lie still.

He glared at the pair on the other side of the bars, now feeling the fury within his chest being stoked.

Who were *they* to laugh at him?

Why should he deserve it?

He had just lost everything he had ever known . . . his home . . . his family . . . *everything*.

The blond girl took a couple of steps forward. She wrapped her fingers around the bars.

She peered through the gap.

Mitts wondered if her wiry frame might allow her to slip all the way through.

"It's okay," she said, "we've got meds—*painkillers*." She paused. "We want to hear some answers from you first, though." She unpeeled the fingers of one hand from the bars and gestured about her. "Had to bring you here, lock you up, don't know if we can trust you yet, do we?"

Not thinking straight, Mitts tried to haul himself up again.

And failed.

Another pair of laughs on the other side of the bars.

Mitts felt his fury building.

The blond girl's smile faded. She fixed her glare onto Mitts, then said, in a cool, calm voice, "So, kid, tell us what happened."

———

At first Mitts couldn't speak at all. He supposed the two of them might take his silence as a sign of disobedience, as if he refused to cooperate with them until they turned him free.

But that wasn't the case at all.

The simple fact of the matter was that he had no idea where to start.

So he went through it all.

From beginning to end.

To what he *thought* had been his death.

As Mitts reeled through his story, he was aware of the sunlight—once beaming in through the letterbox-sized window in the wall—turning to a clear night sky.

Fluorescent lights in the corridor outside his cell blinked to life.

Reminding him of being back in the Compound.

Back in the Restricted Area.

Almost like being home.

Mitts even told the two of them about how he had killed Heinmein. How he had tripped him up. Sent him flying backward. How he had broken his neck.

Mitts said nothing about the creatures.

He left that part out completely.

He didn't see much reason in letting them know about *that* . . .

After Mitts had killed Heinmein, he had worked on some

sort of autopilot, but he had the recollection of pushing the drawer in the Autopsy room back into place, locking it with Heinmein's keys, and then tossing the keys off somewhere in the dirt which surrounded the Compound.

There was no evidence.

Nothing for these two to find.

So he was better off just staying quiet about the creatures.

For now.

When Mitts first began his story, he observed the slightly smug expressions on the faces of his captors. But, as he went on, he noticed the blond girl losing her smirk.

She took on a far more serious expression.

The muscled man's features, too, softened.

When he reached the end of the story, Mitts felt as though he had lived through those seven years all over again.

He wished it hadn't happened at all.

That Heinmein had never come for him or his family.

There was a long period of silence.

Mitts pressed his lips tight together, awaiting his captors' response.

All he could hear was the buzzing of the lights above.

In the distance, he could hear laughter, the clanking of pots. He could smell soup cooking.

. . . *Chicken soup?*

Even if it was all in his mind, his mouth salivated with the thought of the rich, fleshy taste. His stomach emitted a tiny *groan.*

There was nothing he could do to prevent his imagination getting carried away.

The girl leaned up against the cement wall opposite Mitts's cell.

She held her arms crossed over her chest.

With a subtle sidelong glance from the girl, the muscled man holstered his handgun in the waistband of his jeans. He turned his back to them then bashed his fist twice against the door.

It opened wide.

He left the two of them alone.

The girl pushed herself away from the wall. She took a few steps toward Mitts's cell.

She laid her palm across one of the bars.

Mitts made out the contours of her hands.

Lots of callouses.

More than a fair share of bruises.

"I'm so sorry," she said. "I'm so sorry that all that happened to you."

Mitts's throat felt tight. He had an uncomfortable—*too warm*—feeling in his side.

He tried again to rise up from where he lay in bed. But he hadn't the energy to support the pain.

The girl stared at Mitts's side; at the place where he'd been shot. "Just a flesh wound. No fragments I could find— you should be fine once you've had some rest."

She turned her attention up to his eyes.

Mitts felt a faint buzz through his chest.

"You lost an awful lot of blood."

———

The next time Mitts awoke, the muscled man had returned to his cell. He bore a packet of pills. They were all translucent, orange.

He brought water, too, in a plastic cup.

He passed both through the bars then watched on as Mitts took them.

Once he was done, the muscled man swiftly asked for the packet of pills and the plastic cup back. As if Mitts could commit some lasting damage if left with either item any longer than was absolutely necessary.

Appearing from out of nowhere, the girl unlocked the cell door.

She and the muscled man helped Mitts out of his bunk.

Onto his feet.

They guided Mitts along hallways.

In a bleary sort of way, he was aware of staring faces.

Nothing more than eyeballs, gaping mouths—*ghosts* —almost.

They climbed stairs.

Mitts tripped a couple of times.

But the girl and the muscled man held him firmly upright.

Finally, they lay him down in a comfortable bed.

With a firm, well-sprung mattress.

So different from the bland camp bed.

Mitts's room was simple, though it was certainly an upgrade on the cell.

A pinewood door which remained firmly shut.

A large window, left open just a touch.

Thick bars on the outside.

He assumed someone stood guard on the other side of the door, too.

In the distance, he could make out rolling, green hills. Bathed in sunshine.

On the horizon, he could see clumped-up clouds. With dark bottoms.

Would it rain later?

It had been a long time since he had seen rain.

The room smelled strongly of iodine.

Mitts supposed the blond girl had attended to him in the middle of the night, while he was sleeping. When he examined the bandage, he saw it was fresh.

No sign of the copper-coloured marks from before.

Only when Mitts glanced about, did he notice the large armchair.

And that the blond girl, supporting her head on her fist, was breathing heavily.

Eyes closed.

Asleep.

He felt strangely intrusive, staring at her while she slept. But since she was the only animate object in the room, he couldn't help himself.

As if she noticed him looking, she took a final, large breath, fluttered her eyelids, and then blinked away her sleep.

With a yawn, she glanced at him.

She rocked herself onto her feet.

She was wearing the same clothing as the night before.

The dark-green tank top.

The black jeans slashed at the kneecaps.

Dark circles clung to the bottoms of her eyes.

"Well," she said, with a slight smile, turning her back to him and treading over to the window, "did you sleep well?"

Mitts swallowed, still feeling that dry, plasticky taste of the pill he had swallowed the night before. "Were you here all night, in that chair?"

The girl kept her back to him.

She looked out the window, to the rolling hills beyond. "Nice view from here, isn't it?" She squared her shoulders, gave another yawn, then turned to look at him. "This room has just about the best room in the whole Station."

"The 'Station'?" Mitts said.

"Yeah," she replied, looking back out the window. "An abandoned police station. This is our HQ, the centre of this little development we've got going here. Not much more than a hamlet at the moment, I'm afraid, but we're getting there. Certain *factors* make expansion somewhat tricky."

Mitts didn't think it his place to ask her what she meant by 'factors'.

For another thing, he was ravenous.

As if anticipating Mitts, the girl glanced to him, smirked, then said, "I'll go see what I can do about breakfast." She nodded to the wardrobe which Mitts only then noticed. "See what you can do about getting dressed."

————

Mitts hauled himself out of bed, away from the thick, incredibly comfortable duvet.

Within the wardrobe, he found limited options.

In actual fact, there was only one option:

A fairly new, dark-green tank top.

A pair of ragged, clearly well-used, black jeans.

He ditched his soiled jeans and t-shirt.

He pulled on the tank top.

Yanked on the ragged, black jeans.

By the time he had got himself dressed, the blond girl slipped in through the door, with a plastic tray in her hands. There was a cup of smoking coffee on top.

Some scrambled eggs smeared onto the top of a bread roll.

A bowl of cereal with a cup of milk.

Although he had never liked cereal, he couldn't prevent the squirming, groaning sensation in the pit of his stomach.

He was *starving*.

The girl popped out a fold-away table which had stood concealed at the side of the bed.

When she had laid the breakfast tray down on top of it, positioned the table in such a way that Mitts could use the edge of the bed as a makeshift seat, she took up her place in the armchair.

Mitts got through his breakfast in record time.

He even drank down the coffee.

Found that he actually *enjoyed* it.

The liquid seemed to send energising waves through his blood stream. It brought him back from the dour state of mind he had slipped into since finding out about his parents' death.

When he had finished breakfast, he expected the girl to be short with him.

For her to sweep up the breakfast tray.

Carry it out of the room.

To leave him alone again.

But, instead, she remained in her armchair.

Knees pinned together, hands clasped in her lap.

Mitts supposed he was meant to say something, so he mumbled, "Thanks."

The girl gave him a weak smile. "Don't worry about it," she said. "You'll have time to make up for all this hospitality— all this *medical* treatment."

Mitts didn't really want to think about *how* he might be expected to make things up.

"What's your name?" the girl said.

"Mitts."

She wrinkled up her nose, tilted her head to one side. "What sort of a name is that?"

"My parents were hippies." A lump formed in his throat. He swallowed it back. "I don't like to talk about it."

The girl shrugged. She didn't give Mitts her name. "So, listen, *Mitts*, we're thinking about heading up to the Research Centre."

"The 'Research Centre'?" Mitts echoed.

"The place where you were hiding out—with your parents, with that *doctor* of yours."

Mitts felt his chest tighten.

He didn't want to return.

Ever again.

"Don't worry," she said, "nobody's going to ask you to come along with us. You're still recovering. But—"

There was a thudding knock at the door.

Both Mitts and the girl turned their attention toward it.

The door opened a crack. Another girl glanced in. She had cropped sable hair which hung just below her earlobes.

Like the blond girl, and the muscled man, she wore a dark-green tank top.

Battered black jeans.

Well-worn, ankle-high boots.

"Sorry for interrupting," she said, looking over Mitts briefly before turning her gaze onto the blond girl. "It's about loading up the trucks—you sure you want to take all four of them up there?"

"Why," the blond girl replied, "is that a problem?"

The black-haired girl flushed. "Just that Dag says he doesn't think it wise to use up that amount of fuel."

"Well," the blond girl said, "if *Dag* has trouble with me making the decisions then maybe he should think about how he'll win the next election, huh?"

The way that she added a venomous twist to *Dag's* name sent a trill through Mitts's stomach.

The black-haired girl occupied the doorway for another few seconds, glanced at Mitts one more time, smiled lightly, and then disappeared, bringing the door shut behind her.

The blond girl turned back to Mitts, shaking her head. She sighed gently. "Sorry about that," she said, "gets like a mad house here when we bring in fresh meat."

" 'Fresh meat'? " Mitts replied, somewhat alarmed.

"Yeah, when we bring in people we've salvaged every-body about the place wants to get a look at them." She focused her crystal-clear blue eyes on Mitts for a long few moments, and then added, "They all want to get a look at *you*."

Mitts felt himself blush—just like the black-haired girl had, moments ago.

He turned away from the blond girl's stare, pretending to straighten out a crease in his jeans. "What was that she said about an 'election'?"

"Huh? Oh, that." She flicked her fringe out of her eyes. "Just how we run things around here. You see, the first few months—the first year, really—it was madness. No one to lay down the law. Nobody to stop everyone running about the Village doing whatever the hell they wanted. So, we decided to establish martial law. And I got myself made Sheriff—for want of a better word."

Mitts wondered just what the role of a 'Sheriff' entailed . . .

"About the Research Centre, I need to know if there's any threat—if there's anybody present at the facility." She paused, leaned forward slightly. "So, *is* there?"

Mitts shook his head. "No, nobody."

The girl looked him in the eye. "You're sure about that —*absolutely* sure?"

"Yes."

There was a long silence.

Mitts decided he should be the one to break it. "What'd you want to go to the Research Centre for?"

The girl held his gaze. "When we arrived here—to the Village—we scouted the terrain. Closed the perimeter." She pointed past Mitts, out the window, to the hills outside. "Well, we came across that place, what looked like a military facility—some sort of *governmental* building—and, if there's one thing I've learned scalping about these last few years, it's that you want to steer as clear of those places as you possibly can." She shrugged. "We decided to forget the place existed at all—a *decent* policy, let me tell you."

"Why didn't you move away to a different location?"

"Because," the girl went on, "this specific part of the country, this section of landscape, it possesses—how should I say it?—some quite *unique* properties."

"And what're those?"

The girl smirked back at him and then tapped the bridge of her nose.

"You don't trust me?" Mitts fired back.

The girl hunched her shoulders, again looked beyond him, out of the window. "Listen, *Mitts*, the reason that I've stayed alive—the reason *any* of us have stayed alive—is by knowing who we can trust, and, more importantly, who we *can't* trust."

"So you don't trust me?"

"Give it time, Mitts, you only got here yesterday. It'll take time to build a reputation."

"You're going up there—to the 'Research Centre'—to check out my story, aren't you?"

The girl rose up from the armchair.

Mitts rose to meet her.

The girl barked out a command.

Mitts didn't even have time to interpret the words before the door swung open, and the muscled man appeared there, in the doorway.

He held the handgun outstretched, pointed at Mitts's

chest.

Mitts held himself still.

Very slowly, he raised his hands over his head.

The muscled man spoke to the blond girl without taking his eyes off Mitts. "You want me to escort him back to the holding area?"

The girl stepped toward the muscled man, apparently nonplussed by this experience.

"Nah," she said, slipping past the muscled man. "Let him walk around a little. He won't get far—he knows everyone has their eye on him."

And, just like that, the girl disappeared into the corridor outside the room, leaving Mitts alone with the muscled man.

And the gun.

———

Following the showdown with the muscled man—the none-too-unexpected revelation that the blond girl didn't trust him —Mitts decided to remain in his room.

He slumped in the surprisingly comfortable armchair, resting his feet on the bed.

He could feel his temples throbbing. His side throbbed too. He wondered what sort of treatment the blond girl had administered him.

Was she even medically qualified?

What if the wound went septic?

Overly curious now, Mitts reached down and peeled back the bandage just a touch.

He peered down into the open wound.

A dark-red. Some purplish bruising about the edges.

Creaking hinges interrupted his inspection.

He glanced up.

The black-haired girl peeped in around the edge of the door.

She smiled at him pleasantly, glanced about the room, and then said, "Samantha's not here?"

" 'Samantha'?" Mitts repeated.

Only when her name passed Mitts's lips did he realise what it meant.

The blond girl's name.

The black-haired girl, as if she'd just allowed something incredibly delicate—and *exceptionally valuable*—to slip through her grasp, brought her fingers up to her lips.

She arched back her shoulders in surprise, a little like a scolded cat.

Mitts smirked a touch. "You weren't meant to say that, were you?"

The black-haired girl, still wearing her frightened expression, still clutching her fingers to her lips, shook her head.

As Mitts took her in, he realised that she had soft, hazel-brown eyes. She wore a single earring; a spiral of something silver hanging down from her left ear.

Her right ear, he saw, had been torn.

Its lobe was missing.

"I think she's already gone," Mitts replied, finally answering her question.

The black-haired girl nodded a couple of times, but made no move to slip away.

"Do you want to come in?" Mitts asked.

The black-haired girl looked back over her shoulder, out into the corridor behind her, and then she said, "I've got a better idea."

———

Outside, in the *daylight*, Mitts couldn't quite believe he had lived below ground for *seven years*.

It was such a long time.

If he lived to be seventy years old, he would've spent ten percent of his *entire life* down there.

His first concerns about going outside had to do with the fact that none of them wore suits.

When he asked the black-haired girl about this, she shot him a funny look.

As if he was some sort of extra-terrestrial.

She told him there was no danger.

That there was no need for a hazard suit.

That there *was* no radiation.

Not anymore.

Although Mitts wanted to know more, he was distracted by the mere act of walking *outside*.

When they'd emerged out of the Station, and onto the road, Luca—which turned out to be the black-haired girl's name—told him to take care not to trip over any of the loose ground.

And, as Mitts had taken his first steps, he had seen why.

What had once been a—quite probably—beautiful cobblestone street was now dug up all over.

The cobblestones lay about in all different positions. The asphalt layer, beneath, exposed.

All mixed up with earth and sand.

Despite Luca's warning, Mitts stumbled a good few times.

One of the times, Luca had to reach out to stop him falling.

They walked through the dilapidated streets. Past the plaster-walled cottages. The wildly overgrowing hanging baskets. Cracked windowpanes. A few of the cottages' roofs had collapsed in on themselves. It made certain parts of the Village look like a bombsite.

Mitts breathed in. The air was sweet.

It was totally different to breathe in *fresh* air.

So unlike the recycled air of the Restricted Area.

Down there, everything had felt stilted.

Not quite real.

Not even the passing time had felt real.

Mitts assumed he would have to fill Luca in—all over again—about what had happened to him. But, on the contrary, it seemed that she already knew everything.

Word had, apparently, travelled fast.

They trudged along the crumbled-up streets, winding their way upward through the Village. It was when they turned a corner, past a cottage which had a name plate declaring it 'Lily Pond', that Mitts, for the first time, caught sight of the periphery of the Village.

Even if he had had it described to him, he wasn't sure he would've believed it.

From his time pacing through the quiet little village, and looking upon all the houses which were in *desperate* need of being fixed up, he had wondered how this little community had managed to get *so little* done in the time they'd dwelled here.

Now he had his answer.

An enormous wall.

Five storeys high.

Far taller than any of the cottages.

The wall appeared to be made of various pieces of scrap metal, and wood. It was located about a hundred metres out of town. There was a large gate which consisted of a system of wheels and pulleys. It seemed to have been haphazardly patched up with various bits and bobs over time.

A sort of rampart clung to the top of the wall; precarious-looking wooden planks, all hastily nailed together.

Mitts guessed they'd salvaged materials for the wall from the cottages.

That explained why the cottages were in such awful condition.

Mitts looked back to Luca. "This is the way out?"

"And the way in," she said.

"And this," Mitts said, eyeing the top of the wall, "it goes all the way around the Village—protects the entire periphery?"

"Yep," Luca replied, and then, almost out of nowhere—or so it seemed to Mitts—she took hold of his hand. Gave it a squeeze.

Mitts looked back into her hazel-brown eyes. He felt something stirring in the pit of his stomach.

He wondered if he was a little nauseous.

If he was reacting to whatever pills Samantha had given him.

But, no, it was something else.

Luca tugged on his hand, leading him somewhere else. She smiled. "Come on," she said. "I've got something else to show you."

———

They walked for what seemed an awfully long time.

After a while, Luca released his hand.

In the end, the purpose of the walk turned out to be to arrive at a cottage.

One which was located at the very edge of the Village.

The cottage had a thatched roof, turned green with moss. It had scarlet-painted window and door frames. The garden had been kept in a better state than the majority of cottages about town.

"My house," she said, taking him by the hand again, and leading him on.

The two of them headed up the garden path: a sequence of concrete slabs dropped down onto the lawn.

Once inside the cottage, Luca brought Mitts into the kitchen. He watched her as she lit a few gas lamps about the place—it *was* getting a little dark now. She ignited one of the hobs at the gas stove, placing a metal canister of water over it. "Tea?" she asked.

"No electricity?" Mitts replied.

Luca coloured a little. "No, I'm afraid not—we did try for a few weeks, but, well, there were just too many of us to keep the generators ticking along." She reached up for the cabinets above her, flipped open the doors and removed a pair of chipped, white porcelain mugs. "The only place that can really justify twenty-four-hour electricity is the Station."

"I suppose that was one of Samantha's policies?"

Luca blushed even more. "Yes, as a matter of fact it was."

It seemed to him that Samantha had succeeded in placing the Village in an iron grip.

Later, as they sipped at their tea in silence, Mitts listened to the quiet of the Village.

It was incredible.

Nothing like what he remembered of the real world.

No cars trundling back and forth. No people calling out to one another in the street. No aeroplanes soaring overhead.

As he savoured the milky tea, Mitts couldn't help asking Luca if it was fresh.

She nodded in reply.

"Yesterday," Mitts went on, "when I arrived here, I thought I could smell chicken . . . some sort of soup?"

Again, Luca nodded. She placed her cup down on the table, and then pointed off somewhere behind her. "We have farms a little way down the hill. That's where we keep the livestock."

Mitts considered this, that he had been living with his family, down in the Restricted Area, and all this time they had been *so close* to live animals. And their produce.

Mitts sucked down the rest of his tea.

Finished, he stared at the final splash of brown-orange liquid lurking in the bottom.

He glanced up at Luca.

She was in tears.

Surprised, and acting out of instinct, more than anything else, Mitts got up from his chair, went around the table. He crouched down at her side and laid his hand on her shoulder.

As he did so, he felt a slight spark pass through his fingers.

Something he couldn't explain at all.

But it *was* there.

"What?" Mitts said. "What's the matter?"

Luca held herself still for several seconds, but then something within her seemed to let go.

She drew in a rattling breath and then sobbed it out.

She crossed her arms on the table, and then pushed her face into them.

Mitts remained by her side, waiting for her to get over this traumatic response.

Finally, Luca gathered herself together.

She straightened up, looked Mitts in the eye. Her eyes sparkled with tears. "When I heard," she began, "when I heard about your story, about what happened to you, about how your . . . your entire family, how they were . . . *killed* . . ."

Here she broke off for a few seconds, to gather herself back together, to make her voice ring straight and true once again.

She continued, "It reminded me about my own, about my family."

"Did the same thing happen to you?" Mitts replied.

This whole experience felt so surreal.

Mitts knew that he was still in shock over all that had happened; not just the murders of his family. He somehow knew that, over the coming weeks—the coming months and years—it would be a slow process for those wounds to heal.

The scars would always remain.

Luca sunk her teeth into her lower lip and nodded. "Yes, someone . . . someone killed my family."

Mitts reached out and took hold of Luca's hand. She was trembling. He glanced about himself. To the kitchen. To the tiling. To the appliances. Everything had been kept so clean. "Do you live here alone?" Mitts asked.

Luca nodded.

"Doesn't that make you feel lonely?"

Again, she nodded.

It was as if something possessed Mitts then.

His eyes latched onto Luca's.

The gap between their lips closed.

Just as Mitts felt their lips brush together, Luca spoke up.

Her voice was only just above a whisper.

"There's something you need to know."

"Hmm?" Mitts replied, still stuck in a haze.

"Samantha, she protects people. That's what she does. She stayed up with you all night, didn't she? Slept in that armchair beside your bed?"

Mitts drew back from Luca.

He looked into her eyes.

She went on, "She does the same with everyone. Everyone who comes in under the same conditions that you did. That *I* did. The first few times that we brought people into the Village there were . . . there were . . ." here her lips trembled again ". . . *suicides*."

Mitts felt his blood run cold. "You mean, on the night . . ."

166

"Yes," Luca said, cutting him off, "on the night that they were saved, that they were brought here, to the Village, they decided to finish things, that they had already gone through too many changes, that they couldn't *manage* another one."

Mitts held himself still.

He thought about Samantha.

How her snoozing away in that that armchair beside his bed had seemed an almost homey scene.

But now he knew the grisly truth.

Samantha had been worried about him.

Worried that he wouldn't be able to take any more.

Mitts turned back to Luca. "You thought that I might . . ."

"The first night is always the hardest, if it's going to happen that's when it usually does . . . that's why it's important not to leave anyone alone, to make sure they have company. And Samantha takes on that burden for herself."

Mitts really had no idea how to react to this information. What he was *supposed* to do with it. Perhaps he wanted to point out that shoving people into a cell as soon as they arrived to the Village wasn't the best way of putting them into a positive state of mind.

But, catching a whiff of Luca's perfume, he decided to say nothing.

He was certain he had smelled it before, but it was only now—now that he had left behind the sensory overload that had been his milky tea—that he could properly acknowledge it.

Lilacs.

Sweet and clear.

Natural.

As Mitts moved into Luca again, feeling his mouth moisten as he drew closer, she spoke to him, in a voice at a husky whisper. "I'd like to show you some drawings," she said, "of things I've seen."

Right as their lips touched another time, Mitts felt vibrations passing through the floor of the cottage. At first the thunder was distant. And then it was close.

Deafening.

What sounded like a whole convoy of trucks.

Full-sized trucks.

Once again, Mitts drew back from Luca, looked at her with a panicked stare.

What was this?

What was going on here?

But Luca had nothing to say.

Knuckles pounded the front door.

The door flew open.

Someone screamed for them to get down.

A gunshot spat through the air.

Sam America pulled his overcoat hard about his body. The chill of the wind was almost unbearable. It cut him down to the bone. He had been wandering inland for what seemed like months.

Despite the time, he could still taste the salt from the sea breeze.

Could still feel where the sea spray had stripped the moisture from his cheeks.

Whenever he removed his overcoat, and looked down at the stars-and-stripes design emblazoned on his clothing, he couldn't help but see the worn-out material.

Feel a sense of pity.

It would never be quite as brilliant as it once had been.

The worst part of Sam America's journey inland was that he had found nothing—nothing except for the ever-present mud underfoot, constantly slipping beneath the tread of his boots.

It seemed almost as if the world was escaping this reality, and turning to another.

It was days like these—thoughts like these—that made Sam America wonder if the world truly was lost. Was he fighting in a manner which had long ago ceased to be effective?

The village had been unexpected. But, considering that the expected for Sam America was the grim rainy days—the slightly sour, acidic burn of raindrops running down his face—the unexpected was to be embraced.

Sam America trod over scrap metal, wood, all these little pieces that had been salvaged, nailed together —welded together. This had been a last stand, of a sort. One last try for the humans who had dwelled here, in these, surely once delightful, tumble-down cottages.

Sam America walked among the rubble.

He had no idea what he was looking for.

In all his journeying throughout the land, he hadn't found so much as a single soul alive.

Not a human *soul, in any case.*

But he couldn't quite let go of hope.

Because it was all he had left.

As Sam America trod over the broken-up bricks,
listened to glass breaking beneath the tread of his boots,
he heard, over his shoulder, a cough.

Thick, and full, and alive.

COUGH.

COUGH.

SALTED WOUNDS

*C*OUGH.

Mitts flinched awake.

The world seemed to press in on him from all sides.

His brain felt almost numbed.

As if somebody had cracked open his skull and wrapped his brain in cotton wool.

Mitts glanced about him.

The steel bars.

The letterbox-sized window beyond, and high up on the wall.

He was back here.

Back in the prison cell.

As he eased himself upright once more, Mitts felt a slight twitch of pain in his side, from that gunshot wound. But he forced himself up straight. To sit on the

172

edge of the bunk. When the soles of his feet touched the cold floor tiles, he realised that he had no shoes, or socks.

He glanced about his cell, and saw that—indeed—there were no shoes in his cell, either.

He thought back to what Luca had said, about Samantha being worried about the new arrivals going crazy and killing themselves.

Did they think he might attempt to hang himself with his shoelaces?

Now that Mitts took in the cell for a second time—now that he seemed to have his senses together a little better than last time—he noted how he was lying on not much more than a concrete block.

A flimsy mattress laid flat over the surface.

Only a brown, washed-out blanket to keep him from the cold.

He felt his temples pulsing.

He reached up and massaged the afflicted spots with his fingertips. It was what he would do whenever he woke up feeling a migraine coming on . . . usually the result of some strange dream.

Like the one he had just had.

Rays of sunlight gleamed in through the window. As if to torment him, the scent of cooking chicken wafted into his cell.

Even the hint of the buttery water they boiled the meat in

brought the juices rising in his mouth. He could hardly bear to sit still.

So he rose.

Up to his feet.

And he stood at the bars, peering out, as if he might be able to see something—*anything*—at all.

But he was alone here.

Only the objective, uncaring concrete surrounding him.

He reached out and wrapped his fingers about the bars, trying to work out just what had happened. Why he had been brought here. Why that group of armed men, led by Samantha, had stormed Luca's house.

Samantha had given him the run of the Village, hadn't she?

She'd said that he 'wouldn't get far' if he tried to escape.

So why had the reaction been so extreme, so *brutish*?

He reached up and felt the back of his head. He found the spot where one of the men had beat him with the grip of his gun. There was a welt forming there. Just brushing his fingers over the surface sent a shudder of pain through his stomach.

So he stopped.

They had knocked him to the floor.

While he'd lain there, sprawled out, helpless, someone had wrestled him from behind; smothered a damp cloth over his mouth and nostrils.

The smell had reminded him of disinfectant, but it had been stronger.

Much stronger.

It had seized hold of his mind, turned it around and around until it surrendered to darkness.

And to dreams.

The latch on the door jerked.

Its mechanism emitted a fingernail-curling *scrape*.

Mitts breathed in deep—down to his lungs.

He expected to see Samantha appear there, in the doorway, but she did not.

Neither was it the muscled man.

Or—as Mitts had hoped—Luca.

It was someone else.

Someone Mitts hadn't seen before.

Mitts took the man in.

He was quite short.

Stocky.

Tanned skin.

Like everyone else in the Village, he wore a dark-green tank top, black jeans.

But this man's clothes were in better shape than most.

His boots were shined up.

He had a sidearm holstered at his belt.

Unlike the muscled man, who had used the waistband of his jeans to stow his gun, this man had a nice, crisp leather holster for his weapon.

The clasp, which kept the weapon secure in the holster, had been left undone.

Mitts didn't believe this was a mistake.

As the man approached the bars, the door—seemingly of itself—slammed shut behind him.

The man padded toward Mitts, his boots creaking as he went.

He snorted up some phlegm and spat it out.

A blob of spit splattered the floor.

Mitts felt a little of its wet spray against the tops of his bare feet.

As the man stood before him, only a few centimetres dividing the tips of their noses, Mitts breathed in the scent of musk, and of cologne.

He supposed this man took pride in being *masculine*.

"Dag," the man spat.

The man—*Dag's*—glare was intense.

Mitts was so taken off guard he almost missed the outstretched hand sticking through the bars.

He took hold of Dag's hand.

Dag gave him a brutal shake.

At first, Mitts tried not to show discomfort.

Pain.

But, in the end, he realised that he wouldn't be let loose until he'd shown weakness.

Submission.

Mitts flinched.

Dag smirked, then released Mitts's hand.

He turned his back to Mitts and glanced up, casually, to the window above. "Not much of a view, huh?"

Massaging his afflicted hand, Mitts replied, "No, not really."

Dag kept his back to Mitts.

It seemed as if Dag was creating some sort of mental itinerary of the holding area. As if he was worried Mitts might make off with something and he wanted to be able to call him to account.

Finally, pursing his lips, Dag turned around.

In the sunlight, Mitts finally got a good look at Dag's hair, at the tone of it.

A greenish-brown colour which, in the right light, might've been called bronze.

Or *sewage*.

"Listen up, okay," Dag said, "I ain't gonna bullshit you."

Mitts felt Dag's intense eyes on his own.

Dag was several centimetres shorter than he was. But several years older.

Perhaps a few years into his thirties.

He guessed, like a lot of short men, Dag had made a pledge to himself that he wouldn't allow his height to affect him.

He had little doubt that, if he tried anything, he would find himself pinned to the floor in a matter of seconds.

That gun pressed to his temple.

Dag swabbed his tongue about his mouth, picked out something inside his cheek, wadded it into a neat ball of spit and gobbed it out behind him.

At least this time he was polite enough to turn his head when he spat . . .

Mitts stared at the revolting speck of spit on the concrete floor, and then he forced himself to look back at Dag.

"Now," Dag continued, "we went on up to the Research Centre, got the orders that you were holed up there for a good time." He paused, stared into Mitts's eye, point blank. "Correct?"

Mitts nodded.

Dag stared him down.

Mitts realised, for someone like Dag, a nod wasn't an acceptable response.

In the end, Mitts croaked out a weak, "Yes."

Dag went on. "We reached the Research Centre at approximately twelve-hundred hours, and proceeded to scout the perimeter." He glanced at Mitts for a second. "Previously, when we had gone to inspect the Research Centre, we did not know what other kinds of security measures there might be at such a location. So we took the decision to place a DND."

"A 'DND'?" Mitts couldn't help breaking in.

Dag smirked a touch, then gave a slight shake of his head.

He turned his attention downward.

To the tip of his boot.

To a scuff mark.

" 'Do Not Disturb'," Dag eventually stated.

Dag stayed quiet for a long few moments, again fixated by the scuff mark on the toe of his boot.

His smile grew wider, and then, all at once, he snapped his neck upward.

Caught Mitts in his glare.

He thrust his arm through the bars.

Seizing Mitts by the throat.

————

Mitts felt the air slowly being choked out of him.

He felt his chest tighten—his lungs tingling.

His heart seemed to beat slower, as if swelling up.

His vision blurred Dag's features:

His snub nose.

The thin layer of perspiration which clung to his forehead.

Dag squeezed tighter still.

Mitts could feel consciousness leaving him.

Darkness loomed at the fringes of his vision.

All of the visions, all of those dreams, all of them sitting right on the periphery of his consciousness.

Just . . . one more . . . little squeeze . . . that was all . . . all it would . . . *take*.

Without warning, Dag released him.

Mitts dropped to the concrete ground.

He landed with a *thump* on his tailbone.

He felt pain reverberate up his back.

As he sat on the floor of the cell, he watched Dag pace about before him, fists clenched down at his thighs. His fingers kneaded the heels of his hands.

Mitts couldn't help but feel he wasn't the one trapped here.

Dag finally ended his pacing.

He strode back up to the bars.

Gripped them tight in his fists.

"Why didn't you tell us?"

Mitts swallowed.

Pain flashed through his throat.

"Tell you *what*?"

"About the creatures," Dag shot back. "The *Strangers*."

Mitts's mind swirled.

The way Dag said it—the *way* he spoke of them—he could feel the fear.

It had been a long time since he had heard fear in some-one's voice.

Not since he had left home, seven years ago.

Heard his parents' panicked voices.

Dag turned his back on Mitts again. "Our nemesis, the reason why we've ended up like this, strangers in our own home."

" 'Strangers', how?" Mitts replied.

Dag remained silent for a long while.

He gazed upward, to the window, once more.

He squinted as he stared into the direct sunlight.

Mitts caught the impression that he was waiting to see who would be the first to flinch:

Himself, or the sun.

Dag shook his head, then threw up a hand.

It wasn't an act of aggression, though.

More of surrender.

"Aliens," Dag continued, "beings from another dimension, whatever the *hell* you want to call them . . . the point is that they're here, and that things changed . . . *everything changed* when they showed up."

Mitts felt his mind sharpen.

He could feel the strength returning to his body.

His blood seemed to flow with adrenalin now.

He thought of all the questions he had wanted to ask his parents. About *why* they'd had to leave their home. About *precisely* what had happened.

His parents would evade his questions. He had thought it was because there was some deeply disturbing truth that shouldn't bother a *child's* mind.

Now, though, he knew why.

They hadn't known.

Like everyone else, they had seen the news reports.

Panic.

Everywhere.

Doctor Heinmein had offered them shelter.

Told them he could save them.

That he could save *Mitts*.

And so they had gone with him.

What other explanations had they required?

"Come on," Dag said, his voice a little more insistent now, "we've *been up there*, to the Research Centre, we've *seen* the creature in the Autopsy room, near where you snuffed that scientist, doctor guy. You had to have seen the creature." Dag pressed his lips together so hard that all the blood left them, and they turned a faint shade of blue. "Stop *lying* to us."

"I . . . I . . ." Mitts replied, "I know nothing about them—nothing at all. Only what they look like. I saw one, once. We left our home before I knew anything, before my parents knew anything."

Dag tilted his head to one side. "And that doctor, he didn't tell you anything?"

Mitts shook his head. "Nothing."

"I don't believe you."

"I swear that's the truth."

Dag continued to stare hard into Mitts's eyes for several seconds.

Mitts saw something—a vein?—twitch in Dag's eye.

It was almost like watching a thought fire through his brain; the track changing.

Dag continued, "And I bet that chewed you up, huh? Him not filling you in on anything?"

"What?" Mitts said, feeling a touch confused at the turn in the conversation.

Dag smiled slightly. "Yeah, I bet it did, and you couldn't stand it, him not telling you what was going on with the wider world—we saw his studies, those studies on your family; some really *sick* shit."

Mitts felt his heart sink in his chest.

He didn't want to hear any of this.

He didn't want to hear any of this stuff about his *family*.

And, much less, he didn't want to hear anything at all about Heinmein.

Not for as long as he lived.

"That's the problem with scientists," Dag went on, "turn the whole fucking world into some great big science project."

Mitts give his silent agreement.

Dag shook his head and stared down at the concrete.

He was quiet for a long time.

"Wanna know my theory?" Dag said.

Mitts said nothing.

The question was rhetorical.

Dag smirked, half of his mouth rising up his cheek. "I reckon you just lost it totally—flew off the handle." He glanced back at Mitts. "You know that doctor of yours, that scientist guy? He kept a journal."

Mitts shook his head.

"Yeah, he did," Dag went on, "pretty thorough one too, and—my, oh my—did he ever have a whole bunch of bile to spill about you; about your brattish behaviour, your *stealing* those books from that room."

Mitts wanted to protest.

He wanted to defend himself.

But, at the same time, he realised how futile it would be to do so.

Dag continued, "Don't think that we don't realise everything went tits up on your eighteenth birthday." He glanced in through the bars, grinned at Mitts. "Happy *belated* fucking birthday, by the way."

Mitts gritted his teeth.

He glared out from between the bars.

"No," Dag went on, "my theory is that you caught yourself a touch of cabin fever, and that was all it took for you to go crazy, tumble the place the hell over. Kill that doctor, that scientist, your family too."

This time, Mitts couldn't resist.

He felt heat rising up in his cheeks.

Before thinking, he rushed upward, and toward the bars.

He made a grab for Dag.

But Dag was too quick for him.

With a swift couple of steps backward, he was away from the bars.

He pulled his sidearm up and out of its holster.

Pointed it at Mitts's forehead.

As Mitts looked beyond the tiny black hole of the pistol, he saw that Dag was smiling widely.

He was grinning, as if this was just some sort of entertainment.

Dag held the gun on Mitts for another few seconds, before—still grinning all over—he holstered it. He reached up to his chin, and rubbed his fingers through the days' old muzzle of stubble. "Don't you worry about it, though. We can always use a couple of crazies . . . make pretty effective security men in days like these."

With a fat-lipped smile, Dag shook his head and trudged out the door.

It slammed with a steel *clatter*.

Mitts felt himself slip down to the floor.

He could feel the tears well up behind his eyes.

But he pushed them down.

———

Mitts spent most of his time in the cell staring at the concrete wall opposite.

He thought about how the conversation with Dag had gone.

Not well.

It seemed that everyone suspected Mitts was crazy.

That he had killed his own family.

That he had killed Doctor Heinmein in cold blood.

The smell of cooking chicken was too much to bear.

No matter how much Mitts reasoned with himself, told

himself that he had zero prospect of getting anything to eat, he couldn't stop his mouth watering.

He could hear people talking, too, on the other side of the door.

To begin with he had tried to channel into their words, but had found it impossible.

As Mitts sat slumped up on the floor of his cell—resting his back against the wall till it went numb—he tried to think how he might prove his innocence.

He thought about the plethora of cameras back in the Compound.

And immediately shot that idea down.

No power.

It seemed hopeless.

He was the sole survivor.

About an hour or so later, he heard the door creak open.

He turned his attention front and centre, wondering what torture would be coming to greet him.

As it turned out, it was Luca.

As always, she was dressed in her dark-green tank top and black jeans.

He took in afresh her cropped, black hair.

The pinkish glow to her cheeks.

This time, though, she wasn't smiling.

She seemed nervous.

She hung back from the bars.

Mitts's gaze slipped down to her hand. She clutched a

folder; one of those padded ones someone might use for a thin laptop, or for especially important documents.

Luca brought the folder up to her chest and clutched it tight.

She managed a thin-lipped smile, but that was all.

Politeness.

Mitts slid his knees up to his chest and then wrapped his arms around his legs.

He glanced away from her, for some reason unable to look her in the eye.

"Hey," Luca said.

Mitts didn't reply.

He could feel her gaze upon him.

On the air, he caught a slight whiff of lilacs: the perfume Mitts had smelled right before the truck had arrived . . . before he had been knocked to the ground.

Taken away.

"Do you remember the drawings?" Luca said, a slight hop to her voice.

Mitts could tell, even without her standing close, that she was trembling.

She was *terrified* to be in the same room.

Mitts turned his head.

When he spoke, his voice was gravelly. "What're they going to do with me?"

Luca pressed on another smile.

Equally as false as the last one.

"Would you like to see the drawings?" she said.

Mitts glanced to the folder she held in her hand. Then he looked away.

He gave a nonchalant shrug.

As Mitts stared at the grey concrete wall before him, he heard Luca crouch down on the outside of the bars and unzip the folder.

The scent of lilacs was like poison in his lungs. He wished she would just go away. He wished that she would just leave him *alone*. He could wallow here, in his self-pity.

Waiting for . . . whatever they intended to do with him.

"I started about three, maybe four years ago," Luca said, "when I first arrived to the Village. I've never shown them to anyone, until now. I thought that they were just *stupid* dreams, you know? But, for some reason, I feel like I can share them with you. That you won't laugh about them."

Mitts felt like he wanted to roll his eyes, like he wanted to laugh in her face.

Did she not understand what he was going through right now?

How he was locked up for the *second* time since he'd arrived here?

That he was a suspected *serial* killer?

Mitts turned to Luca, looked into her eyes, saw her earnest expression and he realised—right there and then— that he would never be able to speak a cross word to her.

It would be like scolding a puppy.

Mitts turned his attention downward, to the folder. He could make out the pieces of paper within.

Simple sheets of white A4.

Apparently reading his mind, Luca said, "When I got here, I took it out of the photocopier, no one seemed to miss it."

Despite himself, Mitts couldn't help but smile.

There was something so light—almost *childlike*—about Luca's manner.

Then he turned his attention to the drawings themselves.

Luca had drawn them using a blunted pencil.

The first one was awash with grey-black carbon.

Night.

Within the darkness, Mitts made out a pair of figures.

Barely visible.

It took him another couple of moments to recognise them as a man and a women.

Both of them wore party clothes:

The man a tuxedo.

The woman a cocktail dress.

There was a splash of light toward the edge of the picture.

A big party going on . . . off-stage.

Mitts absorbed the picture. Thoughts scattered around his brain.

The details were returning.

The details which, if he'd been asked about them—not

five seconds before—he would've had *zero* chance of recalling.

But he recalled them now.

The smell of the rose garden.

The fragmented song of the string quartet.

The taste of champagne.

That cool, night breeze.

A tingle of excitement as the New Year approached.

A fresh start . . .

But those thoughts—those feelings—none of them came from Mitts himself.

They came from his subconscious.

From his dreams.

He gazed at Luca's face. Her lips were slightly parted. Her eyes wide with anticipation.

She wanted him to confirm, or deny, he saw something in these drawings.

If he *recognised* these drawings.

Luca continued to peel the drawings apart.

More in the sequence.

The sequence of the two dancers which Mitts had observed.

They were out of order, but Mitts put them back together in his own mind.

As far as he knew, the images had come to Luca in a different sequence.

First there was the man in the tuxedo, standing alone on

the balcony, looking out over the garden.

And then the woman appeared in the doorway.

The man turned to her. Looked to her.

The light from inside set her in a silhouette.

The woman stepped toward him.

Darkness rolled in.

And then, in the final picture of the sequence, the pair was totally lost.

To obscurity.

Mitts glanced up at Luca.

He read the earnest expression on her face.

Wanting to know—*needing to know*—that someone else had seen these things.

He gave her a simple nod.

Luca's reply was quick, surely rehearsed.

"I know you didn't kill them—your family."

———

Neither of them spoke after Luca had shown the drawings.

They didn't need to.

Mitts could feel something . . . something he hadn't *felt* before, something throbbing in his inner ear . . . and he knew he had undergone some sort of a change.

That he and Luca had undergone a change.

Because now—*finally*—they had found one another.

Only to be parted again.

Although Mitts wanted to ask about his newest set of dreams, the ones which featured the bedraggled superhero figure—*Sam America*—he couldn't quite muster the strength.

For some reason, if this was to be his final interaction with Luca—before he was unceremoniously tossed through the Village gates, or worse—he preferred to think that they did share some unique connection.

That their dreams were intertwined.

He would cling to a lie over reality for as long as he could.

In the end, there was a knock at the door.

Luca rose.

Before she left, she reached through the bars.

Mitts observed her dainty, pale-white hand. Her fingernails were carefully painted with a clear varnish. He took her hand in his.

Soft skin.

Impossibly soft.

And then—just like that—she left him.

Perhaps forever.

A few hours later, a previously unseen man entered the holding area. Like all the others, he wore a dark-green tank top. A gun was holstered at his waist, like Dag.

He handed Mitts a bowl of cereal, already drenched in milk.

Mitts did his best to act civil. He tried not to let it show that hunger was eating him from the inside out. Under the man's watchful eye, he scoffed the cereal down.

When the man was gone, Mitts was alone again.

It had gone dark outside. The lights blinked on.

The door creaked open again.

This time it was Samantha who stood there.

Mitts felt his heart leap in his chest.

He stood up.

Samantha was alone.

She had no escort.

She stared long and hard at him, as if she was physically trying to see through his lies.

Lies that weren't there at all.

"So," she said, "I see you've met Dag."

Mitts said nothing.

"He seems to have taken a shine to you—despite your lying ways."

Again, Mitts kept himself from saying anything.

Samantha breathed in deeply. Then she said, straight out, "I want you to confirm or deny whether or not you killed your family. And the doctor."

Mitts took a moment.

Allowed himself to get all his rage under control.

He didn't want to mess up what might be his final opportunity.

"It's just as I said," Mitts replied, "I told the truth."

"Apart from the creature," Samantha butted in. "We saw your fingerprints on the drawer in the Autopsy room—bloody fingerprints. You slid that drawer back in, didn't you? Hoping that nobody would see it?"

There seemed no denying it.

Why *should* he try to deny it?

He nodded.

Samantha sighed out a harsh breath. "Why?" she said.

Mitts again took his time. "Listen," he said, "this has been pretty much the most hectic few hours of my entire life. Don't you think you should cut me a little slack?"

Samantha's blue eyes narrowed into slits. "What makes you think we should believe you? That just because you were tired you were incapable of telling us everything?"

Mitts had no answer to that. "I don't know," he said.

Samantha shook her head, and looked about the holding cell, almost with a sense of nostalgia. "Dag's taken a shine to you," she repeated, almost to herself.

And, it seemed, with a deep sense of regret.

"Listen," Mitts said, drawing Samantha's attention back onto him, "I'm sorry for not telling you about the creatures, I . . . I didn't think you knew about them, and I thought that it might freak you all out, that—"

"That we wouldn't take you in?" Samantha said, arching an eyebrow. "And do you think I'd bother staying up all night looking after a new arrival, making sure they don't do themselves in, if you thought we'd cast someone out just because they were a little funny in the head?"

"Well," Mitts replied, "I don't really know—I mean, I *didn't* really know."

"Those creatures are our enemies. That's the reason for the walls—that's the reason *why* we have to live like this." She breathed in, her chest rising beneath her tank top. "You really have no inkling about the world, do you? It's not just a show? Not just a way of making us underestimate you . . . not a means for you to case our living situation before turning it to your advantage?"

"Look," Mitts replied, "I've lived underground for the past *seven years*, why don't you just assume that I've got about as much knowledge of the outside world as an extremely advanced new-born baby, huh?"

Samantha met him with a stern glance. Her precise, sharp blue eyes followed him.

She was looking for any sign of defiance.

Anything which might topple the balance.

She nodded, seemingly to herself, and then made for the door.

But Mitts wanted to know one more thing. "What did you mean when you said that I wouldn't get far if I tried to run? Did you mean that I wouldn't ever make it past the Village gates?"

Samantha froze. She didn't turn, remaining in profile.

Mitts got a good view of those three scars on the side of her face.

All three of them were *deep*.

"No," she replied, finally, "anybody is free to come and go as they choose. We never cast anybody out. What I meant to say was that we're on a peninsula. This place, where we find ourselves, is one of the last habitable locations on Earth . . ."

Without further explanation, she slipped out the door.

Leaving Mitts to his thoughts.

———

The car engine churned.

Mitts stared into the headlights of the oncoming cars.

All of them gridlocked.

Halted.

But their side of the road was clear.

They were going the wrong way . . . they *had* to be going the wrong way.

He looked to the driver.

To the grey-haired man driving.

And then he looked to the back seat.

To his mother.

She sat huddled up against the window.

Her eyes were closed. But Mitts could tell she wasn't sleeping.

His father sat up front, beside the grey-haired man.

The grey-haired man was driving quickly.

Mitts heard his father speak.

"Are you sure about this?"

"Yes," the grey-haired man replied, "they shall all be dead by daybreak—this is the only way out now."

Mitts's stomach went all gooey.

His heart sunk.

Something . . . something about the situation. It just didn't feel right.

Mitts was so used to his parents—to *adults* in general—being a calming influence.

But now they seemed to be the source of tension.

The grey-haired driver took the next corner sharply.

Mitts's parents' case slipped from one side of the car boot to the other.

It bashed up against the sides with a heavy *thunk*.

The car drove on.

Mitts felt himself being gently lulled to sleep.

When he next opened his eyes, it was to see the sun already rising on the horizon.

Setting the sky in its pinkish-orange glow.

He looked to his parents. Both of them were sleeping.

The grey-haired man continued to drive.

As Mitts sat alone, on the back seat, looking over the grey-haired man's shoulder, he recalled the shuddering sensation passing through him.

The knowledge that things would never be like they were.

Mitts followed the transition from deserted motorways, to winding, single-lane country roads.

He listened to the *rustle* of long grass against the side of the car.

When the car pulled to a stop, his parents were awake again.

Before their eyes stood the Compound.

The wire fence.

The flat, square buildings.

The grey-haired man scanned his plastic card against a reader. A *bleeping* sound emanated from somewhere. The hefty wire gates retreated, groaning back on their hinges.

When the car came to a stop, all of them got out.

All of them yawning . . . except for the grey-haired man:

Doctor Heinmein.

They worked quickly, unloading the boot.

The large case.

Mitts grabbed hold of his sports bag: the one which contained every last worldly thing he owned.

The rest was gone.

Later on, perhaps the one time Mitts successfully managed to corner his father—to drag something of an explanation out of him—he got something of the real story.

Heinmein had warned of the danger. He had told Mitts's father he had a safe place for his family.

But they couldn't bring others.

There was no time.

Not enough *space*.

But Mitts knew, from the calculations he had performed, that they could've saved more.

Many more.

But Heinmein had had to have his experiment.

He had had to play his games.

Take his notes.

Turn Mitts and his family into lab rats.

Ones which would never escape.

He had lied to them.

Bred fear.

And then, when his controlled conditions were threatened, he had panicked.

Shown his true colours.

Made that final—*fatal*—transition from scientist, to maniac.

Why had Mitts been the only one to see?

———

The next day, Mitts watched the golden sunlight glisten through the window. It reached its most brilliant just before nightfall, when it faded and turned back to darkness.

He wondered if everyone in the Village had forgotten about him.

Or if, maybe, some sort of crisis had taken place.

Meaning that Mitts had been relegated to some secondary task.

He didn't know which of the two eventualities he would've preferred.

What he did know was—about an hour after the lights had blinked on; after he'd chewed through some cardboard-tasting cereal—there was a sudden and high-pitched siren.

It was shrill and it seared through the air.

It was so out of place in the otherwise *tranquil* location of the Village.

Mitts snapped upright, straight-backed, like a soldier standing to attention.

Outside the window, he heard a commotion, the stomping of boots.

Panicked shouting.

Dag appeared in the doorway.

His eyes were crazed, his smile more so.

He held what looked like a rifle.

"You doing all right?" Dag said, striding up to Mitts's cell and—without a word of explanation—opening it with a large key.

Mitts stared at Dag, watching as he freed him from the cell.

For a long while, Mitts stared at the opened door, as if Dag might be teasing him.

He was certain that, in a matter of seconds, Dag would bring it shut.

With the flash of a smile.

Perhaps a dry chuckle.

But Dag made no move to shut the door again.

In fact, he turned a touch impatient.

"What're you waiting for?"

Mitts felt a little dizzy as he left the cell behind. "Where're we going?"

Before Dag replied, Mitts found a rifle placed in his hands.

It was much heavier than Mitts expected.

He almost dropped it.

"You'll see," Dag replied.

Sam America had spent hours searching for the location of the cough.

But he found nothing.

It was only in his mind.

He could feel vibrations passing through the ground.

An earthquake?

No, he didn't believe so . . . but, then again, what made him say that?

This was still a natural world.

It still possessed the same features it had had when humans roamed the face of the Earth; when they had been the dominant race.

Before the Strangers had come.

The sky was growing grimier now as Sam America paced through the broken-up village, with its cobblestones all turned up, and the shoots of trees and grasses ground up through the exposed earth.

People had lived here once—survivors—but they were long gone now.

Of course they were.

Everyone *was* long gone now.

Anyone with any sense.

As Sam America paced past the dilapidated cottages, the broken windows, the tumbled-in roofs, he wondered whether the people who'd lived here, who'd survived *here*, had found some happiness.

Because in this grey, grim world, he thought that the rarest of things.

Sometimes he wondered if something so abstract as happiness would ever be possible again.

But he tried not to think on that too frequently.

It wasn't his responsibility, after all.

His brief—where it began, and where it ended—was to salvage what he could of the human race.

Nothing more, nothing less.

Then his task would be through.

Then he could be said to have been a success.

THE HUNT

Mitts *felt a hard slap* on his shoulder.

"You still with us, pal, or what?"

Mitts blinked away his daze.

Dag was staring back at him. "Seemed to slip away there for a moment."

Mitts shook his head. He reached up and pressed a finger to his temple. "Yeah," he said. "I think I'm okay now, though."

"All right, if you say so," Dag said, looking at him from out of the corner of his eye and then trotting on.

Mitts stumbled several times as he tried to keep up with Dag.

There were others with them, maybe a dozen, perhaps a few more.

Mitts could hear their well-drilled marching boots all around him.

When Dag had led Mitts out of the Station, they had proceeded through the Village at a rapid pace, and out of the gates. Then they had ended up on the stodgy, uneven earth which they were attempting to navigate now.

To begin with, Mitts had been almost overwhelmed by the thick, rich scent of wet earth.

It had been so long since he could recall being surrounded by it.

So long that he had assumed he would never experience the sensation again.

A steady drizzle fell.

It soaked Mitts's tank top.

But he felt no cold.

That was the thing about the Village.

About the whole surrounding area.

The temperature was so comfortable.

Nobody ever wore jumpers.

Nobody ever wore anything more than the dark-green tank tops and the black jeans.

Right now it was humid.

Mitts felt his shirt stick to his skin. His drooling sweat mixed with the tumbling rain.

Several times, Dag grabbed hold of the front of Mitts's tank top. Keeping him on his heels.

He wondered if Dag had been instructed to keep a close eye on him.

Or if Dag—just by instinct—wanted to have Mitts nearby.

At first, Mitts had been afflicted by a gnawing numbness in his legs. That was due to him having been kept in a prison cell for several hours. It took him a short while to get over the sensation.

To refind his legs.

Another issue was the rifle. Mitts wasn't used to its weight and it caused him to lose his balance several times. With each step forward, Mitts would almost feel himself ready to trip over.

To land in the muddy earth with a *squelch*.

He clung onto the rifle tightly. Mostly out of fear.

There was no way of knowing what Dag would do if he lost it.

They finally reached their destination.

Heavy, lurking mists clung to the ground.

Obscuring everything.

Mitts observed the others around him get down on one knee. Take aim with their rifles.

Point off into the mist.

It took Mitts a moment to realise what the mists concealed.

Water.

All around.

A lake?

The sea?

A peninsula . . . that was how Samantha had termed it.

On instinct, Mitts glanced about him, to Dag.

Dag had drawn his rifle.

Like the others, he was down on one knee.

Dag eyeballed him. "You gonna take up your position or what, pal?"

Dag didn't wait for Mitts's reply. He simply reached up, grabbed a hold of Mitts's shirt and dragged him down onto the sodden earth.

Mitts listened to the sharp *clicks* and *snaps* as the others prepared their rifles.

"How'd I do it?" Mitts said, unable to keep quiet any longer.

Dag, his attention back on his rifle, and his focus concentrated on the sight, said, "What'd you mean?"

Mitts stared hard at the side of Dag's face, waiting for him to look back at him.

Finally, he did.

Dag fixed him with a stern glare. "You don't know what you're doing, do you?"

He yanked Mitts's rifle out of his hands, made it give a hard *snap*, and then passed the weapon back.

As Dag crouched back down into his ready position, he peered out into the mist, shaking his head. "Thought you killed your family . . . and now you don't even know how to prep a gun."

Before Mitts had the chance to reply, one of the armed guard among them called out.

Mitts turned his attention forward.

To the mists before his eyes.

Out there, in the obscurity, Mitts heard a throaty, sustained:

Croak.

———

Shots went off all around him.

Mitts's heart hammered in his throat.

There was something about the *crack* of the shots which sent a shudder down his spine.

Something about *that* sound which set him on edge like nothing else.

Was it the knowledge that his whole family had been dealt with using gunfire?

Or was it something deeper buried?

Mitts was still staring off into the mist when he felt a sharp elbow in the ribs. He turned to see Dag there, nostrils flared, mouth a gaping hole. "Come on then!" Dag said. "You gonna shoot or what, nutbag?!"

Mitts glanced down, to the rifle he still held in his hands. And then he looked off, along the barrel, and into the mist.

In imitation of the others surrounding him, he brought his rifle up, and peered along the sight.

All he could see, though, was mist.

Nothing else.

Out of the side of his mouth, right after Dag sent an earsplitting shot through the air, Mitts said, "Where're we aiming?!"

But Dag was back to concentrating—concentrating on something which Mitts couldn't see.

Dag prepared his next shot. "Just shoot!"

With the *crack* of Dag's latest shot ringing about his skull, Mitts brought his own rifle up. He felt its weight. And then, with a tentative finger, shaking hard, he squeezed gently.

Mitts felt the vibration rattle his bones before he heard the reverberating shot, and, even then, it sounded to his ears as if it had come from another gun.

Allowing the rifle to fall in his grasp, Mitts looked out into the mist, as if it might give him a better idea of what he had just shot.

But there was nothing.

Nothing *he* could make out.

Again, though, over on the bank, someone shouted.

The gunshots ceased.

Mitts felt panic ripple through those assembled on the bank. He felt himself shudder hard and long. A shudder he couldn't control. Not even by sinking his teeth into his lower lip.

There was a moment of disorder—of *confusion*—among the men.

Mitts looked to Dag.

When Mitts glanced around, he realised that everybody else was doing the same.

Looking to Dag.

Waiting for their next move.

"Fuck!" Dag said, staring off into the mist.

Mitts followed his gaze, unable to understand what the problem was.

But then he saw them.

Their shapes forming out of the mist.

Slipping in between the sheets of never-ending drizzle.

Even in the night, by the light of the moon, Mitts could make out the shade of their grey-purple flesh. The slightly wet quality to their skin. And then, with the coolness of the night-time breeze blowing against his cheeks, Mitts caught that overpowering stench of sulphur in his airways.

Mitts stood captivated by the sight.

By how they *floated* over the water.

How their limbs hung down at their sides.

Dancers slinking effortlessly across an ethereal dancefloor.

Coming toward them.

Coming to greet them?

When Dag screamed out his next order, it was loud enough to send a quiver all the way down to the soles of Mitts's feet.

"Re*treat*!"

———

Mitts ran blindly forward. He hoped he was headed in the right direction.

Headed back to the Village.

Several times, he glanced back over his shoulder.

He caught sight of them.

Their bodies *floating* through the air.

Even despite the situation—despite the obvious peril— Mitts cast his mind back to what Doctor Heinmein had said. How he had concluded that the Strangers moved across land by 'dragging' themselves.

His hypothesis had been wrong.

As Mitts bounded onward, at Dag's side, he heard the odd *snap* of gunfire on his heels.

He breathed in deeply, already feeling fatigued, despite his exercises, all the work he had put in with his routine back down in the Restricted Area.

Between gulps of air, Mitts managed to form words.

"What . . . are . . . *they?*"

Dag bounded on beside Mitts.

He saw the slight look of fear in Dag's eyes.

That *childlike* fear.

The one which drove Dag toward safety.

Which *implored* him to return to safety.

A matter of life or death.

Mitts glanced back. The others had kept themselves compact.

Some turned to shoot into the mists as they retreated.

Dag shook his head, grabbed hold of Mitts's shirt and dragged him onward. "No fucking idea, but we've gotta kill them."

Mitts said nothing more as they closed in on the gates of the Village.

Gently, gradually—*too slowly!*—the gates were opening.

Dag only slowed when they passed through the gates.

Only when Mitts was standing back on the broken streets of the Village did he feel safe.

Safe from the monsters outside.

The Village was deserted.

Dag was barking out yet more orders.

Finally, he turned to Mitts.

A look of frightened decisiveness glared out from his eyes.

"You!" he said to Mitts. "Get up there, on the rampart. *Now!*"

Mitts obeyed.

He tagged along behind the others as they hauled themselves up the ladder.

Mitts reached the top.

About a thousand splinters jammed into his palms.

He glanced about the fear-stricken faces.

All of them staring along the barrels of their rifles.

Underfoot, he tried not to think too much about the precariously hanging, nailed-together, wooden boards. Most of the planks were half rotten.

Clearly structurally unstable.

Not up to the task of supporting this many people.

But there was no choice.

They *had* to be able to see out.

Over the walls.

Below, Mitts observed the gates to the Village gradually being swung closed.

Out there, in the mists, he could hear someone shouting out.

One of *them*.

He turned to the others around him.

To those with rifles clutched in their grips.

Some of them were women, he noticed now.

The short haircuts and the uniforms unsexed them all.

"You hear that?!" Mitts said. "There's someone out there! Someone who didn't make it in!"

Not one of the stony faces, their eyes fixed to the sights of their rifles, responded.

Once again, Mitts felt his heart in his throat.

Tickling his tonsils.

He looked down.

Caught sight of Dag.

Thick in conversation with Samantha.

Knowing what he had to do, Mitts rushed along the rampart.

Some mumbled curses at him, but Mitts paid no attention.

He could feel his chest tight. His rifle butt knocked against his lower back.

He hurried his way down the rungs of the ladder.

This time he felt the splinters sink deeper into his skin.

Pain throbbed in his hands.

Finally, he landed on the broken-up cobblestones.

He turned his attention to Samantha and Dag.

Before he could get out so much as a word, Dag's wild-eyed glare turned on him.

"I told you to *get the fuck* up there, on the rampart!"

Mitts felt his pulse pound through his body.

He held himself still.

He met Dag's burning-eyed gaze.

Kept his calm.

He responded in a clear voice. "There's someone out there—I heard the screams."

"Get back up!" Dag replied.

Mitts held himself still. "We have to open the gates."

The cooling, night-time rain still drooled down.

A stench of sulphur cut through the air.

He felt Samantha staring at him in profile.

He slipped her a brief glance.

Took in her pert-lipped expression.

He got the impression Samantha had been telling Dag the same thing.

They had the same idea.

Dag gave Samantha a hard glare.

He turned his back.

Trotted away from them.

"Please!" Mitts called out after Dag.

But Dag's only response was to wave an arm in the air.

Mitts met Samantha's blue eyes.

He saw the sorrow.

The despair.

Then he heard the hard, rusted-up hinges of the gates creaking into life.

———

Mitts stole out through the tiny gap in the gates.

Back out into the mist.

He could still hear the voice.

The cries for help.

He glanced back over his shoulder.

Samantha stood there.

She disappeared as the gates slammed shut.

Five minutes.

Dag would hold his gunmen off for *five minutes*. Once that time passed, they would shoot at anything that moved outside the gates.

Mitts trudged across the sodden earth.

He raised his head, listening out for the screams.

Only now did he truly realise *why* everybody in the Village lived in fear.

Why they lived in a fortress.

An outside enemy.

Something which threatened them.

Strangers.

He wouldn't forget the look of fear on Dag's face for a long time.

Back in the holding area, Mitts would never have believed Dag capable of showing fear.

Not in company.

Mitts held his rifle up.

He stared through the sight.

Into the mist.

Looking for those shapes.

The ones which'd indicate the *creatures*.

The Strangers.

But he saw none of them.

He reached up.

Wiped the rain out of his eyes.

"Hello?!" Mitts called out.

He listened for a reply.

Ears primed.

Ready to head off in any given direction.

No response.

Mitts wondered how long had passed.

He wondered how many of those five minutes he still had.

He called out again.

"HELLO?!"

This time Mitts heard something.

". . . Over here!"

Mitts jarred his head around.

Stared off into the mists.

He could make out a form.

He headed toward it.

As he drew closer, he made out features.

A man maybe five or six years older than he was.

Bald.

His rifle lay off beside him.

On the earth.

His leg had slipped down a hole.

Got stuck.

The man brought Mitts's face into focus.

He broke out into a maniacal smile.

"Thank you!" he said, in accented English, and then, "Thank you! Thank you!" as if this outpouring of gratitude was where their struggle ended.

Mitts shouldered his rifle.

He looked over the man.

How would he do this?

How would he do this?

The man was heavy-looking.

Surely twice Mitts's weight.

Mitts crouched down. Ready to help the man free himself.

He had seen the man before.

He vaguely recalled having seen him in the kitchens.

Back at the Station.

Mitts got closer to the man. He reached out to take hold of his outstretched hands. He caught the thick scent of roast chicken clinging to him.

A warm pang passed through his chest.

Mitts clung on tight to the man's hands.

He summoned all the force he could.

Pulled.

He wouldn't budge.

A sudden flush of giddiness passed through him.

Nausea.

Apparently noticing Mitts's struggle, the man's eyes widened.

He pointed over Mitts's shoulder.

His mouth yawned open.

Revealing a dark pit within.

Mitts followed the man's finger.

Looked past those well-chewed fingernails.

Out beyond.

There Mitts saw them.

Hundreds of them.

Drawing close.

Appearing out of the mist.

Mitts breathed in.

The air felt cold now.

Much colder than it had before.

His skin puckered into goose pimples.

The sound of croaking filled the air.

Surrounded.

They were *surrounded*.

Creatures appeared out of the mist on all sides.

No escape.

Mitts turned his attention back onto the man.

His lips shook.

He was jabbering away.

About something or other.

Prayers?

Mitts listened in closer.

The man's voice was almost a whisper.

"Don't leave me, don't leave me, don't leave me . . ."

If Mitts ran now he might save himself.

Surely he had another minute to make it back.

Another minute before Dag ordered his men to recommence shooting.

He looked up, to the creatures again.

They loomed large in the mist.

He took in their faces—their *expressions*—for the first time.

In the Autopsy room, back at the Compound, the specimen's face had been bloated.

Almost comical in appearance.

Now, though, there was nothing *comical* about their

wide, beady black eyes.

Or their spiderlike fangs.

Or the spittle which hung down from them.

Either side of their torsos, stubby, whale-blubber growths hung off them like obese human arms.

Sulphur filled the air.

The bitter scent of urine.

He glanced back to the man.

His leg stuck in the hole beneath him.

His eyeballs swivelled about their sockets.

Mitts grasped hold of his rifle.

He stared along the sight.

But there were too many.

He *knew* there were too many.

It would be a worthless attempt.

As his finger rested against the trigger, Mitts felt something swill through him.

It reached his gut.

He felt the strength in his trigger finger give in a touch.

He knew that he *must* fire . . . that he had to put up some sort of a fight . . . and yet, he just couldn't.

Already, it was too late.

He was surrounded.

An unbroken chain.

Mitts breathed in the sulphuric air.

He took it down into his lungs.

He thought back seven years, to when he had been in the Restricted Area.

Heard the rain pattering.

The sound of it carrying along the air vents.

He thought about the scent of disinfectant:

The room with the overalls.

He thought about the looks on his parents' faces when he had found them:

Dead.

When he'd found his little sister, Floo:

Dead.

And *dead* was just how Mitts was going to end up.

He strained his eyes to look into the mist as it closed in on the two of them.

Could he see their faces?

His family?

His mother . . . his father . . . Floo . . .

Mitts breathed the sulphuric smell right down to his bones.

His knees buckled.

His mind ebbed free of consciousness.

He landed with a distant, damp *thud* on the sodden earth.

Sam America stood on the fringe of the little, tumble-down village. He cast his glance over the place another time. As he had walked out, to the edge of town, the clouds had bundled up into blackened cotton wool.

The rain had started to fall.

It fell heavily now.

Sam America knew he should find shelter.

What good was a superhero with a head cold?

He turned his back on the village for a final time, putting the place to rest within his mind, never to be thought of again except—perhaps—in unexpected dreams.

Then he heard it again.

Cough.

Cough.

Cough-cough.

Sam America cast a glance back over his shoulder. He took in the rubble, the fallen cottages. He attempted to string together just where the sound had come from.

Cough.

Cough.

Sam America shifted from his spot, now certain of where he had heard the coughing. He strode hard, through the rubble. Over the broken cobblestones. As he drew closer, he heard heavy, bothered breathing.

The kind of breathing—Sam America knew; from experience—led to a speedy death.

He crouched down and worked quickly at the rubble. He grabbed hold of the chunks in his muscular grip. He tossed them away.

Sam America tore another couple of rocks free. And he found himself staring into a pair of eyes—eyes which caught what remained of the daylight.

Hazel-brown.

Blond hair.

Pale—pale—skin.

A boy.

A MIRACLE

Mitts *thought* he might be suffering from déjà vu when he awoke.

Once more, he heard those whispering voices.

And—once more—he had had those strange dreams.

The ones with that superhero.

With *Sam America*.

Mitts could see the redness of the sunlight up against the backs of his eyelids. He pried open one eye, and then the other. He was back in the room he had been taken to after he'd been 'relocated' from the holding cell.

On instinct, he glanced to the armchair beside his bed.

It was empty.

For some reason, he felt his heart sink a touch.

He had expected Samantha to be there, of course, but she wasn't.

Still, he supposed he should've been glad to find himself *not* in the holding cell.

He turned on his side, pushing the duvet away. He realised he was dressed in only his boxer shorts.

In addition to those whispering voices, Mitts could smell coffee.

Its odour wafting about.

The door flew open.

Luca, bearing a tray of steaming scrambled eggs, appeared in the gap.

She smiled lightly at him as she trod inside.

She didn't bother to close the door behind her.

He looked out into the corridor.

A white-washed wall. Smudged with marks.

"Good morning," Luca said, with a smile.

She seemed more carefree than she had in their last meeting.

Maybe it had to do with the milieu, with the fact that he wasn't in the holding cell this time.

Or perhaps it had been their impromptu bonding session over the drawings.

The ones which'd shown Mitts he wasn't alone . . .

Luca set the tray down on the bedside table. He eyed the cup of coffee he'd smelled from before. Her lilac perfume had replaced the odour of coffee now.

Mitts thought about the bitter taste of coffee. Back in the Restricted Area, it had made him want to puke. Now, though, his body needed the caffeine to survive.

The eggs were white and fluffy—heavy on milk and black pepper—just how he liked them.

How had she known?

Had she . . . read his thoughts somehow?

Luca leaned over him, kissed him on the forehead. She blushed a little.

Mitts blushed too.

She rounded the foot of his bed and sat on the armchair. "Hero's breakfast," she said.

Mitts sat up, propping himself on his elbows. He felt somewhat exposed to only be in his boxer shorts. To be here, in the bedroom with Luca—*bare-chested.*

He felt a pair of stabbing pains in his skull.

He screwed up his eyes and reached up to his temples.

Laid his fingers over the pain.

Massaged.

"Don't remember?" Luca said, still smiling.

Her lilac perfume caused Mitts's nostril hair to tingle.

Breathing it in made the inside of his chest itch.

He strained his mind. Tried to dreg up the memories.

That only made the pain in his skull all the more intense.

He shook his head.

Luca combed her fingers through her smooth, sable hair.

She wore a pink ribbon in her hair. It brought out the colour in her cheeks.

"When the mist cleared Dag sent men out there," Luca

said, dialling her smile down. "Thought that it'd be an expedition to bring back a pair of bodies—we *all* thought that."

The pain in his skull grew so intense that he began to shake. He had to *do* something. So he reached out for his coffee. Took hold of the warm cup. Sipped at the bitter liquid within.

He glanced back to Luca.

She continued.

"Dag said you'd both passed out; that you were lying on top of Yuvna."

" 'Yuvna'?" Mitts said, taking another sip of coffee and then feeling another pair of stabbing pains at his temples.

Luca nodded. "The chef—works here, in the Station. Portly guy."

Here she puffed out her cheeks and made a waddling motion with her arms down by her sides.

Despite his headache, Mitts couldn't help but laugh.

He pulled himself back from his giddy outburst. "Is he okay?"

"He's *fine*," she said. "A little shook up, but who isn't shook up these days?" She smiled faintly, then went on. "I guess the two of you had quite some introduction."

Feeling the pains come on harder now, Mitts placed his coffee back down.

He breathed deeply.

Lay back in bed.

"Don't want your eggs?" Luca said.

"Later."

"Not feeling too good?"

"It's just this"—another stab at both temples. Mitts winced—"*headache.*"

Luca leaned into him.

Placed her pleasantly cool palm across his forehead.

"When they brought you back this morning there wasn't a scratch on either of you. But you were both burning up. Like you'd got some sort of fever." Luca jerked her thumb in the direction of the door. "You should've seen Samantha, she had her med supplies out, and everything. She was even talking about sticking you with a drip. To give you back some of the fluids you were sweating out."

"Yeah," Mitts said, feeling his heart give a slight jump, "I'm feeling pretty dehydrated."

Luca got up from the armchair and then disappeared through the door to the en-suite bathroom.

She returned bearing a jug of water and a glass.

She poured then handed the glass over to Mitts.

He took it with extreme gratitude.

He touched the glass to his lips. The water felt like an elixir.

He drank the whole glass down in a single gulp.

Luca poured him out another one.

He drank that one down too.

She poured a third, adding, in admonishment, that he 'take it easy, this time'.

Mitts did.

He took a sip and replaced the glass on the bedside table.

When he looked to Luca, he saw she was gazing out through the window.

Out to the rolling hills beyond the Village.

"What happened to the creatures?" Mitts said. "Did they . . . just *go*?"

Luca breathed in deeply.

Her chest puffed up.

Then deflated.

She glanced to the door.

Perhaps she was under instruction to leave out certain details.

"Luca?" Mitts pushed. "Please?"

Luca's smile faded completely now.

She met Mitts's eye briefly. Then her gaze shifted out the window again.

When she spoke once more, her tone was steady, almost robotic.

"The creatures," she said, "they were surrounding you— you and Yuvna. When Dag and the others saw them, they . . . they opened fire."

Inexplicably, Mitts felt a rising heat within his chest.

It pounded at his cheeks.

At his temples.

Although the migraine remained, it became only background noise in his skull.

Mitts hoiked himself upright in bed, leaned against the headboard. "They did *what*?"

Luca shook her head. She clutched her hands, laid them in her lap and then stared.

"There was no choice."

"No choice?" Mitts said. "What'd you mean? Of course there was a choice. You said it yourself, we were still alive, they weren't *doing* anything."

Luca wouldn't meet his eye now. "You have to understand, Mitts," she said, "what they've done before."

"What *did* they do before?"

Luca held herself very still.

She was breathing in deep, apparently trying to get her head together.

Trying to work out the best way to put what she had to say next.

She took so long to respond that Mitts convinced himself he would have to prod her into an answer once again.

But then, finally, she did reply.

A film of tears made the surface of her eyes appear glassy. "You don't understand. They *kill* . . . they've *killed* everyone they've come across."

Mitts felt the headache scale back a little.

His brain felt like mush.

As if it'd been kneaded over and over again.

He felt almost as if a void opened in his chest.

"You called me a hero when you came in." He paused for a moment, and then added, "Why?"

Luca didn't look away from Mitts this time.

"Anybody out there—anybody who's ended up facing those creatures—they've been killed . . . you, though. You and Yuvna . . . you survived."

Mitts felt himself sinking down into the mattress.

He closed his eyes.

Tried to see off the wave upon wave of pain which afflicted his tired mind.

———

Although Mitts sincerely dreaded it, he decided that he couldn't stay inside his room for the rest of his life. That he would have to face the others eventually.

As he dressed—in the dark-green tank top, the black jeans —he heard muttering outside the door. He'd only just got himself dressed when there was a pair of short, sharp knocks.

He didn't have a chance to tell them to come in.

They just barged right through.

Mitts surveyed the figure standing in the doorway.

The man from last night.

The man he had 'saved'.

The chef, Yuvna.

He took in his large frame. His stomach sagged over the

waistband of his jeans. His bald head was buffed to a shine. A chef's hat balanced precariously on his scalp.

He wore a well-stained apron over his dark-green tank top.

The straps of the apron were almost lost to the mass of his neck.

Just like the night before, a scent of roast chicken clung to him.

For several seconds, Yuvna fixed Mitts with a stern glance.

Mitts was half expected Yuvna to take a swing at him.

But then, all of a sudden, Yuvna broke into a wide, toothy smile.

He tromped toward Mitts. Something jangled in his pockets as he threw his enormous arms about him. "My hero!" he said, sounding genuine enough.

Not knowing what to do, Mitts waited for Yuvna to get through with the hugging.

After about ten seconds, Yuvna pulled back.

He continued to beam at Mitts.

His blue-grey eyes swivelled about in their sockets.

"I never believed," Yuvna said, speaking with a foreign accent, as he had the night before, "that someone would come to help me. I thought that I was dead."

"Well," Mitts replied, "I didn't really do anything . . ."

Yuvna pinched his lips together into a pout.

Frown lines wrinkled his forehead.

He tilted his head slightly. Waggled his finger at Mitts.

"No, no, no! You *saved* me. There should be no doubt about that."

"Okay," Mitts said, with a slight smile, feeling a touch beleaguered by this whole experience.

"Tonight," Yuvna said, taking a pair of steps back, toward the door, "tonight I shall cook up a feast that you shall never —ever—forget." He grinned at Mitts. "Tell me, tell me, what is your very favourite dish?"

"I haven't had hamburger and chips for a while."

"Hamburger," Yuvna replied, grinning all over, "and *chips*."

Yuvna clapped his hands together, like a court jester tickled by an especially witty joke.

As he stomped out of the room, hands clasped, he muttered quietly, under his breath, "Yes, hamburger and chips. Hamburger and *chips*."

And then, without another word, he was gone.

Only when Mitts heard the large man's footsteps disappear off down the hall did he allow himself to relax.

Before he left the room himself, he glanced both ways to ensure Yuvna was really gone.

He couldn't be too careful.

————

The Village gates were open.

As Mitts passed through, he expected the guards standing by to stop him.

But they only gave him a knowing nod.

Once he was out of the Village, and treading along the rolling, green hills, feeling the gentle suckle of the damp earth beneath him, and breathing in the cool breeze, he could almost imagine that he was back to the time before.

To the time he recalled from childhood.

Before everything had changed.

Mitts glanced to the large, concrete structure up on the hillside.

As he walked, he couldn't take his eyes off it.

As if the spotlight might blink on at any second.

As if Heinmein might not really be *dead*.

Although he hadn't taken the time to plan his route, he found himself soon walking toward the stretch of water. He thought about what Samantha had said—about how they were on a peninsula.

He wondered if he could really believe her.

Could he *trust* her?

Would she *trust* him?

He thought back to the meeting with Luca.

She had mentioned that Samantha had been looking in on him.

Making sure that he was doing okay.

Luca had said this attention wasn't personal.

That Samantha would've done it for anybody.

He was nothing special.

And yet . . . and yet, the night before . . . however much he wanted to fight it, it was apparent that *something* had happened.

Something which Mitts could never have anticipated.

Judging by all the reactions, the feast coming that evening, he had achieved something which, quite simply, had never been achieved before.

Mitts walked along the water for a long while.

He stared off across the glassy, grey surface.

When it got dark, Mitts decided he'd better be getting back to the Village.

He might not be able to find his way *home* if he went too much further.

Not at night.

He paced back toward the dim, orange lights of the Village—the ones which hung about the perimeter of the wall. He felt the incline of the hill in his calf muscles.

He listened to the sound of cows lowing.

The clucks of chickens carrying on the wind.

The snorts of pigs.

Homey sounds.

Sounds which, he'd believed—in the stark, unnatural light of the Compound—he would never hear again.

They soothed him.

Calmed his aching head.

Dulled his migraine to a low-level throb.

As he continued back to the Village, he noticed something else.

A small, fenced-off area. Just to his right.

About a hundred metres from the gates to the Village.

Curious, he approached the fenced-off area.

As he drew closer, he saw that the fence was made—like everything else—of cast-off corrugated iron, pieces of wood nailed together, large rocks stacked up.

He glanced about, wondering if there might be somebody nearby. If he might be intruding on some place with a private purpose.

He scolded himself for thinking that way.

What was going to be so private that they'd decided to leave it way out here?

More than likely this was just a dump. Where they left all manner of rubbish from the Village.

Mitts glanced about the fence, trying to find the way in.

Soon, he found it.

Nothing more complicated than a busted door lying across a gap in the nailed-together wooden planks and corrugated iron strips.

He prised it back and walked through.

Into the fenced-off area.

As Mitts trod over the stodgy land, again feeling the mud suckling at his boots, he made out vague shapes in the fading light.

It took him a moment.

240

And then he realised what the shapes were.

Small, wooden crosses.

They stood up out of mounds of earth.

In horror, Mitts turned his attention downward.

To his feet.

He was standing on a grave.

Quickly, he took a backward step.

Shifted off.

He stood to the side, in the long grasses.

He'd knocked a cross over, too.

He crouched down.

Straightened it back up.

"They killed them all."

Mitts's heart leaped against his ribs.

He pivoted around.

Stood nose to nose with Samantha.

He reached up to rest his hand over his rapidly beating heart. "You scared the life out of me."

Samantha gave him a slight smirk. She flipped on a torch.

A powerful, blue-white beam dazzled Mitts.

He held his forearm up to guard against the glare.

"Sorry," she said, "that was immature."

"*They* killed them all?" Mitts said.

"Uh-huh."

Samantha glanced about the graveyard.

Her eyes passed over the anonymous, small wooden crosses.

Mitts looked back at her. "You don't sound that . . . well, *sad* to say it."

Samantha continued to look over the shallow graves.

She sniffed once.

Twice.

Mitts wondered if he might've pushed her to the edge. If she might burst into tears.

But she didn't.

Her gaze remained strong.

Unmoved.

Finally, she looked back into Mitts's eyes. "There's no time to be sad," she said. "I've lost everything already—I've cried all that I need to in my life. What's the point in crying some more?"

Mitts felt a knot twist in his gut.

A chilly breeze blew across them.

He breathed in.

And then out.

"I don't smell salt," Mitts said, changing the subject. "That means we're not by the sea."

"No, we're on a lake, in the middle of a mountain range." She glanced back at him. "One of the most remote places on earth."

"Yes, but *where?*"

She shrugged. "I don't know—*nobody* knows." She sighed out strongly. It was almost as if she was expressing some sort of disappointment at the deceased's fates. "When it started to rain—when it didn't *stop* raining—we just drove, and drove, and drove . . . we crossed oceans, or at least large rivers." She glanced briefly at Mitts and then looked away, smirking. "To be honest, I slept most of the way."

"What about those people you came with? Are they still alive?"

She shook her head. Turned her back to him. "Nah."

Mitts thought she might be crying—*silently*—but when she spoke again, her voice was hard.

Firm.

If she *was* crying then she was doing an extremely good job of hiding it.

"Come on," she said, "we should be getting back. Don't want to be late when you're the Guest of Honour at your own feast, do you?"

Mitts gave a subtle sigh. "I guess not."

Samantha led the way. She opened up the gate to the graveyard, watched Mitts through. Stood over him, almost like an overprotective mother.

Then she closed the gate behind them.

Mitts remarked at how smoothly she walked.

At how she hardly moved her shoulders at all.

How she held her chin upright.

Proud.

He supposed she had spent a lot of time cultivating her image.

And she must've exercised a lot of energy in maintaining it.

She couldn't allow it to drop.

Not for one second.

They closed in on the Village gates.

Mitts felt something spark in his mind.

On impulse, he reached out and touched Samantha lightly on the shoulder.

She flinched.

A little taken aback by her reaction, but unabashed nonetheless, Mitts said, "I know where you got those scars."

Samantha continued to stare forward—toward the Village.

She didn't look back.

"Do you?" she said.

She whistled.

And the gates opened for them.

———

Mitts could hardly believe it when he stepped in through the Village gates.

He had thought, at best, a feast might mean a rather noisy gathering in the kitchen of the Station.

Everyone with a plateful of something.

Lots of merry chatter.

Well, there was *lots* of merry chatter, all right.

But he hadn't expected the streets to be packed..

He hadn't expected a series of wooden benches to have been erected over the dilapidated streets.

All of the benches covered with tablecloths.

He recognised one of the 'tablecloths' as curtains from the Station.

Already, people sat at the benches.

Drinking from cups of all kinds.

Speaking animatedly.

Laughing.

Hardly having seen a soul in the past seven years of his life, Mitts had to admit that he felt somewhat overwhelmed.

He hadn't thought there were this many people in the Village.

It was then he realised Samantha had slunk off.

That he was alone.

Before he had the chance to slink away himself, a trio of drunkards approached him.

Two men. And a woman.

"Oi!" the woman said, her tank top showing off her large cleavage. Her breath *reeked* of what Mitts supposed was alcohol. She held a shaking finger accusatorily out at him. "Last night, it was *you* who saved him." She closed one eye as if she was having trouble focusing. "Weren't it?"

Mitts looked to the two men; one on either side of the woman. "Uh," he began, and then, not seeing a way around this, responded, "Yes, that was me."

This caused a roar among the trio.

All three of them bellowed something or other.

Liquid splashed out of the cups they held in their hands and onto the ground.

Before Mitts could escape, one of the men grabbed him by his shoulder.

He pressed a cup to his lips. "Drink! Drink!" he barked at him.

The others joined in.

"Drink! Drink! Drink!"

Mitts felt the liquid running down his chin.

It sent a tingling sensation dancing across the surface of his skin.

Although he tried his best not to drink any of the liquid down, he felt the burn of it in his mouth.

He tasted its *sour* flavour.

More than anything else, he wanted to spit.

But he knew, with these watchful—*drunken*—eyes on him there was no prospect of that.

It might be interpreted as an insult.

And, although these people were drunk, they surely didn't *deserve* to be insulted.

Mitts took some of the liquid down. It sent quivers through his whole body.

He felt it swill all the way down to the pit of his gut.

He looked to the happy, drunken faces.

Saw their smiles.

When the man removed his hand from his shoulder, Mitts took the opportunity to peel away from the group.

As Mitts made his way through the crowds, past all the grinning faces—all the words of congratulations—he felt overwhelmed.

He had deserved *none* of this.

Sure, he had gone after Yuvna. He had located him. But he had done nothing at all to protect him from the creatures.

All Mitts had achieved, it seemed, was those creatures' deaths.

The *Strangers'* deaths.

Finally, he picked out Luca, sitting on one of the benches.

She sat opposite a guy Mitts had never seen before.

As Mitts sat, the guy gave him a wide smile.

Then reached over the table and grabbed hold of him with a two-handed handshake.

Another few 'well-dones' later, and Mitts turned his attention onto Luca.

She smiled gently. "I came by to look for you earlier, but I couldn't find you."

Mitts could feel the liquor heating up his stomach.

It caused blood to rise in his cheeks.

"I decided to take a walk," he replied.

Mitts breathed in the smell of cooking meat.

Beef.

He glanced about, trying to locate the source of the smell.

His nose led him to the Station door.

Yuvna emerged—*grinning*—bearing a tray with an enormous hamburger and a large serving of chips.

Before Yuvna had come within twenty steps, Mitts caught that thick, greasy odour.

He could feel his whole body *crying out* for the morsels which Yuvna brought.

"For my *hero*," Yuvna said, setting the hamburger and chips down on the tablecloth.

At the back of his mind, Mitts wished Yuvna wouldn't call him that.

Mitts regarded the food before him.

The lightly floured bun with poppy seeds.

Melted cheese leaking out around the edges.

Fluffy, crispy chips.

Smothered in salt and vinegar.

His mouth watered.

When he looked up, he realised that everyone's eyes were fixed on him.

Yuvna stood over him—hands clasped—waiting for Mitts to deliver his judgement.

Mitts didn't want to disappoint.

Finally, he shovelled his fingers beneath the hamburger bun. Felt the warmth of the meat passing through his fingertips. As he held the hamburger right before his lips, he found his stare drifting, off across the crowds. He picked out Samantha.

Standing there.

Her blond hair pulled back into a ponytail.

She eyeballed him.

The only face that *wasn't* smiling.

When Mitts felt Yuvna's firm grip on his shoulder, squeezing him—*imploring him to have a taste*—Mitts broke off eye contact with Samantha.

Turned his attention to the hamburger.

And took a large bite.

Sam America bent down over the boy.

The hazel-brown eyes.

The blond hair.

He reached out his hand.

The boy took hold of it.

As Sam America helped the boy free, up onto his feet, he couldn't help noticing that it wasn't a boy *at all.*

No, this was a man.

When Sam America spoke, his voice was thick and gruff. Just how he liked it. Since he hadn't had the need to speak with anyone in so long, he had forgotten how much he loved the sound of his own voice.

"Y'kay, son?"

The man stood very still. He was breathing in and out very rapidly. Something about his features put Sam America in mind of a baby bird. And yet those biceps of his . . . Why, they were pretty much fit to burst.

Sam America glanced beyond the man. "Any other survivors? Any more buried here, underneath the rubble?"

The man just stared on beyond Sam America, gazing off over his head, as if there was something in the distance which Sam America had no ability to see.

When the boy spoke, his voice was so monotonous—so numbed by pain, or something—that Sam America almost missed the words.

". . . No," the man said. "Nobody left—nobody alive."

A single tear rolled down the man's cheek.

Sam America gripped the man's shoulder.

Gave it a tight squeeze.

"Ain't no shame, son. Ain't no shame."

The man tilted his face up to him.

"Who are you?"

"Who am I?" Sam America replied, jerking his thumb at his chest.

A smile broke out onto his lips.

"Why, son," Sam America replied, "I'm just your garden variety superhero, that's all."

He smiled wider.

"At your service."

PART 3
A TORTURED MIND

Smart footsteps clack along the corridor.

Bright, white lights.

A smell of sulphur rips through the air.

Catches in the throat.

Hammering pulses.

Pounding skin.

A female figure in a white lab coat.

Clean. Neatly ironed.

Long red hair drapes down her back.

A scientist.

The footsteps cease.

The scientist pauses at the keypad.

Taps the numbers. No thought. All muscle memory.

A pair of flat tones.

Two blinking red lights.

Then a single—subtle—flash of green.

The door slides open.

Smooth, soundless.

The scientist treads through the doorway.

Into the darkness within.

AWAKE, AT LAST

Mitts *could hear* Luca's heavy breathing.

Breathing which told him she was sound asleep.

She wouldn't be aware of anything until she woke in several hours' time.

He had to make the most of it.

Bare-chested, wearing only pyjama bottoms, he slipped on the bedraggled pair of flip-flops he used as slippers.

The flip-flop straps had been repaired—*hundreds of times* —using scraps of elastic bands.

Occasionally, when Mitts was walking along, minding his own business, one of the elastic bands would snap. There would be the initial pain. The snapped elastic pinging against his skin. Then there would come the stumble—the fall.

And he would smash into whatever blunt object happened to be nearest.

He glanced over his shoulder, about the darkened bedroom.

The shapes of their *things*.

A chair covered with dirty laundry.

A wardrobe which contained dark-green tank tops, pairs of black jeans.

He cast a quick glance out through the thin bedroom curtains.

Out across the Village.

The night kept everything still.

Out on the landing, he took care to avoid creaking floorboards.

He could make out the faint odour of chicken casserole on the air. What Luca had prepared earlier that evening. It had been delicious. The pastry flaky. The meat buttery and smooth.

One of the best things he had ever tasted.

It had left him with a warm, fuzzy feeling inside.

A feeling which'd lasted until his dreams had come.

Mitts eased himself down the staircase. He put all his weight on the banister.

When he reached the bottom of the stairs, he paused.

Held himself still.

He listened out for Luca's breathing.

That gentle, *predictable* rhythm.

Five years.

Five years they'd been together.

It was hard to believe.

Almost as long as he had spent in the Compound.

Down in the Restricted Area.

And so different.

Although he was twenty-three, he didn't feel all that different to when he'd been eighteen.

Of course he was a little older, but was he any wiser?

His horizons hardly expanded beyond the Village.

Every day, it felt as if Mitts had only escaped the Compound to arrive here.

Another prison.

The cottage wasn't all that large.

Upstairs there was a bedroom, bathroom, and what Luca liked to call the 'box room'.

Satisfied Luca was still sleeping, Mitts shifted along the bare wooden floorboards.

He guided his way about various obstacles:

A hat stand thick with splinters.

A rotten hole in the floorboards.

Downstairs, there was the entrance hall, a kitchen, a toilet, a sitting room.

And a study.

It was the latter which interested him tonight.

Mitts trod into the study. He felt a tingle pass down his

spine. A slight, swirling nausea entered his blood. Something within told him that he was doing something *Wrong*.

That he was *invading* Luca's privacy.

Although Luca would always say that her home was *his* home, Mitts could read the subtext.

He knew that this room—*the study*—was off limits to him.

And yet it was the most interesting room in the house.

Because here—he believed—he would find answers.

Moonlight floated in through the window.

The air smelled of furniture polish.

A large, oak desk sat in the middle of the room; a piece of furniture clearly designed with a much bigger space in mind.

Mitts turned to the bookcase.

What he had come for.

What he *always* came for.

Well-thumbed books occupied the lower shelves—novels and manuals, mostly.

He turned his attention upward.

To the higher shelves.

Mitts ran his fingers along the spines of the folders.

He got about a third of the way along the shelf.

And then stopped.

He pinched the folder.

Slid it out.

He took care to do so silently.

He glanced back over his shoulder.

For some reason he caught the feeling he was being watched.

He wasn't.

Mitts paced over to the oak desk. He laid the latest folder down flat.

He raised his head, listening for any stirring within the house.

Hearing nothing, he zipped the folder open.

His hands were shaking.

He could feel his heart pounding a little harder.

Palms sweating.

Because he knew it could be here.

That, what Mitts had just seen in his own mind—in his *dreams*—might be drawn out here, in visual form.

Among Luca's dream logs.

———

Mitts peeled back the pages. He took a few seconds to consider each drawing before turning to the next. Each time he turned the page, he felt a sudden, inexplicable excitement.

Some hope that the next drawing would be the *one*.

About a year ago, Luca had stopped sharing her dreams with him.

Every year, a day-long party was held in the Village.

A party dubbed the Mid-Summer Blowout.

A chance for everyone to let down their hair. To drink their moonshine liquor.

To get intoxicated.

As a matter of principal, Mitts hadn't ever got involved.

But last year had been different.

On the night of the festivities, Mitts and Luca had had an argument.

Over what Mitts didn't remember.

All he could recall was that he had stormed out of the house.

Determined to have a good time.

He had made a beeline for the Station.

He had met up with the others.

All the others involved in the Patrol.

They were surprised to see him, of course, but that didn't mean they weren't *delighted*.

Over the years, Mitts had built up something of a reputation for being a sharpshooter. For being one of the most valuable members of the Patrol. He was the one who, more often than not, managed to spot the Strangers out there, in the mist.

He would guide the group's shooting.

Although not one to brag, it was impossible *not* to hear the rumours about town.

They said *he* was the reason for nobody having been killed in the Patrol in recent times.

Mitts didn't think this down to any sort of skill.

At least it was nothing he was *consciously* responsible for.

On top of his well-publicised 'heroics' five years ago, this made Mitts one of the most popular people in the Village.

His mates in the Patrol would implore him to join in with the Mid-Summer Blowout. Each and every time Mitts would volunteer to take watch. He had never had a thirst for liquor.

That night, though, he had changed his mind.

Before he knew it, his fellow Patrol members had tipped what felt like gallons of liquor down his gullet.

Mitts could still, to this day, recall how the whole world had swilled and swirled beyond his eyes.

How Yuvna had had to prop him up so he wouldn't topple over.

Later that evening, Mitts had puked his guts out in one of the Station toilets.

Even now, a year later, he could still recall the sting of bile at the back of his throat.

How it'd felt like a never-ending stream pouring right out of him.

He had come to sometime around dawn.

Still in the Station toilets.

Someone had been standing in the doorway. As he had peered through his blearily focused eyes, he had squinted hard, trying to make the silhouette out.

Somewhere, in his bleary brain, he had decided it was Samantha.

And so he had spoken her name.

It was only when Luca trod forward, closer to him—her

features becoming obvious—that Mitts realised it wasn't Samantha after all.

Luca had taken him to bed.

In their bedroom, with the next day dawning, she had turned her back to him.

Drifted off to sleep, without a word.

The next day, at breakfast, she had brought a damp, warm towel for him to lay over his forehead. Over a strong cup of coffee, he had tried to explain. He had attempted to jabber some explanation about Samantha always being there to protect everyone.

That she was *always* cropping up like that.

But it hadn't helped.

Ever since then, although there were flashes of their relationship—of the former romance—Mitts knew, in reality, it was over.

Trust had been breached.

There was no turning back.

And it mattered not at all that Samantha was dead.

———

The sun shone in through the study window.

Mitts felt its warmth.

Dawn.

He flipped the next page over.

It felt as if someone had punched him right in the

forehead.

He glared at the page. Unable to understand.

What was he *seeing*?

He squinted.

It wasn't one of Luca's meticulous pencil sketches.

It was full colour.

He took in the details.

The man dressed in a royal-blue top hat.

White stars speckling it.

A white, cotton shirt underneath.

Bright-red suspenders.

His dream.

This was his dream.

The one which he had had years ago now.

He stared hard at the page.

And then he turned it over.

A comic strip.

A page that'd been torn out of a comic.

He glanced up, to the title at the top of the page:

SAM AMERICA: A NATION AWAITS ITS HERO

Mitts leaned back from the desk.

The chair squeaked a little beneath his shifting weight.

"Couldn't sleep?"

Mitts's heart skipped a beat.

He jerked around to look.

Saw Luca standing there.

She wore her white nightie. Her sable hair tumbled down over her shoulders.

He read her expression.

No anger.

No disappointment.

Had she expected this?

Had she *known* what he had been up to?

Mitts swallowed hard, then said, "You saw him too—in your dreams?"

Luca held Mitts's gaze.

Her cheeks had once held a pinkish glow, but now they had turned a richer red colour.

From working out in the sun.

That had been another innovation of the past year, or so. Luca had opted out of Patrol rotation. She had decided she preferred to work in the fields.

'Womanly work', as she put it herself.

To Mitts, though, there didn't seem all that much *womanly* about field work.

Luca crossed her arms. She tilted her head to one side. Smiled faintly.

He could hardly remember the last time she had looked at him that way.

With tenderness.

He wondered if what he'd done, in reading her dream logs, hadn't been some sort of validation for her. He had shown that he *did* still see value in her.

That they still shared their connection.

"Come on," Luca said, still smiling. "I'll make us some breakfast."

Mitts remained where he was, at the table, the folder still open before him. That comic strip of Sam America spread out. "At the end," Mitts said, "when you last saw him, in your dreams, was he walking through the Village—the *destroyed* Village?"

Luca's smile faltered.

Her expression darkened a touch.

She broke off eye contact.

"Yes," she replied, in a quiet voice.

"One more thing," Mitts said.

She glanced up, briefly, her smile now completely gone.

The familiar darkness resting just beyond the surface of her eyes.

"The last time—the last time you *saw* him—was he digging someone out of the rubble?"

"Yes," she repeated, her tone deadpan.

"And," Mitts continued, "was the person he pulled out . . . were they . . . I mean, was it *me*?"

Even as Mitts said it, he felt like a total idiot.

Just who did he think he was?

But Luca shook her head.

"No," she said, her voice not much more than a *croak*. "It was me."

Mitts felt his chest tighten.

Before he could say anything else, Luca turned away.

Disappeared into the kitchen.

———

That evening, Mitts headed out with the Patrol.

Like always, he thanked Luca for dinner. He leaned in and kissed her on the cheek as she tended to the washing-up. Sometimes Mitts tried to help out with the housework but, more often than not, Luca would reprimand him for doing so.

As if it wasn't his 'duty'.

Once outside the Village gates, with his troop of ten or so, he felt all his muscles seize tight.

He looked over his men.

He was responsible for all these people.

Responsible for getting them back home safely.

For some reason, before tonight, that fact had never *really* hit home.

He glanced up, to the rampart.

He looked to Dag—an eyepatch now covering his left eye —and gave him a salute.

Dag saluted back, stern-faced, and then, the crutch under his arm, limped away.

Out of sight, down below the wall.

Mitts headed his team, led them across the rolling hills, the squidgy earth.

It was hard to believe how things had changed.

How Mitts had gone from being a dangerous—possibly *deranged*—prisoner to heading up the entire Patrol once Dag had been incapacitated.

The same night Samantha had died.

As Mitts led his men across the terrain, directing them to take up positions with the motion of an arm, he found himself stumbling back in time.

Three years ago.

That was when it had happened.

It had been a Patrol just like any other.

Wasn't that how traumatic things *always* occurred?

On a 'normal' day . . .

They had laughed—*joked*—as they'd prepared their weapons.

He and Samantha had ended up in a room together.

Alone.

They'd been forced to make polite conversation.

Forced to *pretend* there was nothing between them.

Sometimes Mitts wondered if Samantha herself noticed the spark.

Sometimes Mitts was convinced the spark was there for anybody to see.

For anybody who *wanted* to see.

Out in the mist, Mitts heard croaking.

He snapped his mind back to the present.

He tasted sulphur on the air.

The smell of *them*.

The Strangers.

The mist moved in over the water.

He felt a slight chill.

Another few *croaks* . . . it reminded him of frogs calling.

His men knew what to do.

They took up their positions. Gripping their rifles tightly.

Taking a knee in the sodden earth.

Staring down their rifle sights into the mist.

Mitts waited for the creatures to come. They always did.

As he felt the chilly, white clouds of mist wash over him, his mind ebbed back to that fateful evening once more.

It was so much like it was now.

The mist rolling in.

Croaks filling the air.

A dim awareness that Luca was close by.

That she was grinning at him in profile.

Like all of them, with a false sense of confidence.

Like it was all just a game.

As if nobody could come to harm.

In retrospect, everything was primed for something careless to happen.

And that was just how it played out.

Mitts recalled the minute details.

His eyes had left Luca's.

He had traced the shore.

All the way down.

All the way back up.

Samantha and Dag had been about a hundred metres off to the left.

On the lower ground.

Mitts recalled distant concern. Thinking to himself about how, whenever the two of them occupied the same space they seemed to forget who was in charge.

Either consciously, or by some unspoken agreement, Samantha *or* Dag came out on Patrol.

Never both.

But a stomach bug had struck down many of the Patrol.

Replacements were required.

Mitts had turned his attention back to the incoming mist.

Turned his attention to priming his weapon.

To being ready for the creatures to attack.

When the first few shots had rung out in the night air, he had thought nothing of it.

All his attention had been fixed upon listening out for the *croaks*.

But there would be no more *croaks* that night.

The creatures, for whatever reason governed them, decided against coming that night.

Mitts heard screams for help.

Down by the shore.

He recalled leaving his position. The first to do so.

He had launched himself down the slope.

Knowing there wasn't a second to waste.

At one point, he lost his balance and fell into the water.

As he drew closer, approaching the screams, he felt the mist moving in around them.

A quiver ran through his stomach.

He was afraid of what he would find.

Mitts had seen Dag first. Had seen the blood pouring down from his left eye.

He was lying on his side.

His rifle nowhere to be seen.

Despite Dag's state, Mitts had moved quickly.

He demanded to know where Samantha was.

Dag had pointed off in the direction of the water.

Mitts had glanced back over his shoulder. Seen Luca there. Standing open-mouthed.

With no time to think, Mitts dumped his rifle and threw himself into the water.

He had never had much practice at swimming.

It was forbidden for any inhabitant of the Village to swim because of the creatures.

Despite that, though, Mitts had kept himself afloat.

He had pushed himself into a doggy-paddle.

Once he'd got ten, fifteen metres out, he had glanced around.

Trying to see something—*anything*.

He had seen a string of bubbles.

He had dived down.

Even now, pacing out on the muddied earth two years

later, he could still feel the sharp pain—*agony*—which had accompanied his dive.

He shook his head at the pain and stared off into the mists.

He felt a gentle, warm drizzle falling against his cheeks.

A throbbing sensation passed through his gut.

It pulsated upward, almost inevitably directed for his skull.

He breathed in deeply.

The way he did when he woke from nightmares.

He swallowed the sensation back down.

Turned his attention back to the mist.

They would be coming soon.

And he had to be ready.

Otherwise he would put everyone in danger.

The day after the Incident, as they'd come to refer to it, Mitts had led the search for Samantha.

They had all trod through the water, looking for her.

But there had been no trace.

The night of the Incident, a doctor had gone to work on Dag.

Between winces of pain, and screwed-up eyes, as the doctor worked at his bloodied leg and eye, Dag had filled him in on the details.

About how Samantha had come out of the dark at him.

How she had shot him in the leg.

He had only defended himself, bringing his rifle butt up.

Slamming it into the side of her head.

She had stumbled back.

Into the water.

Gone under.

The following day, when they'd gone in search of her body, they had only uncovered her boots.

Washed up on the shore.

Mitts had stayed there, at the water's edge, for so long.

But he had seen nothing at all.

It seemed he would be forever haunted by her ghost.

———

"Incoming!" someone called out.

Mitts glanced down.

Saw where the man's finger was pointing.

Into the mist.

Mitts steeled himself. Propped his gun up.

Prepared.

Something was wrong—the *air* was wrong.

Mitts wondered if he was getting a cold.

If his nose was blocked.

He couldn't smell their *sulphur* scent.

He felt a tingle in his gut.

The feeling that *something* wasn't right.

His men began to fire.

Their bullets pelted through the mist.

Into the night.

Mitts held still.

He didn't squeeze his own trigger.

He raised his arm.

His men ceased fire.

They stilled.

Down on one knee.

Guns pointed out into the mist.

Mitts listened closely. It wasn't *croaking*.

Finally his mind wrapped around the sound.

An *engine*.

That was what it was.

He peered long and hard into the mist, trying to make it out.

But he couldn't see a thing.

At first he mistook it for moonlight.

Then he realised what it was.

A spotlight.

Yellow, and bright, and sweeping through the mist.

Mitts rose up.

He trudged down the soggy earth. To the shore.

He shouldered his rifle—for which he would've scolded a younger member of the Patrol.

He could make out its shape now.

A *boat*.

At first it looked enormous. Too large to even contemplate.

But then it became smaller.

The mist swirled away from the craft.

The spotlight beamed across the shore.

Mitts shielded his eyes with his hand.

He could hear voices from the boat.

Shouting.

His men closed around him.

All of them staring at the sight.

At the *boat*.

The boat came to rest. Its engine clicked off. It moored a little way off shore.

Some of his men waded out into the waist-high water.

Their rifles forgotten.

Mitts held back.

He wanted the high ground.

Where he could see *everything*.

Where he had a *complete* view of the situation.

He knew nothing about these people.

They could be aggressive. They could be a *threat* . . .

They could be—

She clambered over the side of the ship.

Into a dinghy.

He saw her just as clearly as he had seen her the night of the Mid-Summer Blowout.

A ghost.

Samantha's ghost.

A light blinks on.

Darkness recedes.

Shadows scurry for the corners.

Dozens of glass capsules. Lined up in a row.

Their metal fixings glare in the light.

The scientist treads over to one of the glass capsules.

She reaches out.

Presses a button.

A hiss of escaping air.

The capsule's glass steams up.

It renders the contents of the capsule impossible to see.

The scientist works quickly, with precision.

She busies herself with the contents of the capsule, her

hands tending to the body within as if it were as tender and delicate as a human baby.

As the steam clears, the contents of the capsule is revealed.

Grey-purple skin.

The texture of whale blubber.

Gleaning dully in the light.

The jaws.

The fangs.

All trace of life gone from the black, black eyes.

RESURRECTION

*A*t *breakfast the next day*, Mitts stared long and hard into his cup of black coffee.

He had just polished off his second cup and he could already feel the unpleasant sensation of caffeine overdose rippling through his bloodstream.

He stared at the browned dregs at the bottom of his cup.

He swilled them about, like tea leaves.

He tried to see something in them.

Wasn't that the point of being psychic?

Of having visions?

Weren't they supposed to . . . tell him *something*?

In an unthinking act of frustration, he gripped hold of his mug and hurled it hard against the kitchen wall.

The mug broke apart with a high-pitched *tinkle* of breaking porcelain.

Feeling his heart beating hard against his ribs, and the pull of his strained breathing, he stared at the broken pieces lying on the floor.

The brown splodge on the wall where the cup had made contact.

As he sat at the kitchen table, he heard Luca's footfall on the staircase.

He didn't turn his head when he sensed her standing in the doorway.

"I don't want you in my house."

Although her words were so clear, so gently delivered, they felt like knives rammed in beneath his shoulder blades.

The caffeine rattled through his body.

It caused him to shake.

He was afraid.

Never before had he shown any hint of aggression.

Not even while fighting the creatures.

And certainly not inside the Village . . . much less within Luca's cottage.

He glanced to Luca now.

Standing in the doorway.

Her eyes were set on him. Her lips pursed.

She turned her back to him, heading up the staircase.

Her words floated to him over her shoulder.

"You have till nightfall," she said.

For a long few moments, Mitts stared hard at the broken pieces of his coffee mug.

Then he shifted himself up from his seat.

Left the cottage behind for good.

————

The Village was alive with activity.

Today, everyone had forgotten their duties.

Nobody tended to the farmyard animals.

There was no one manning rations storage.

Not even a soul—apparently—staffing the Station.

And it was all because Samantha walked among them again.

A pair of men dressed in uniforms escorted her.

They wore uniforms from *before*.

Their uniforms were navy blue. Each had a silver tag pinned to the breast pocket.

A tag which Mitts couldn't read.

Their trousers, also navy blue, had been neatly pressed.

Just like everyone else, Mitts found himself staring at them.

He was unable to believe these people were real.

They were fantasy creatures.

He examined their well-muscled arms. The semi-automatic rifles they carried.

Mitts took in the array of reactions from the inhabitants of the Village.

Some scowled. Others looked worried.

Others still smiled and laughed.

Shouldn't they all have been smiling and laughing?

For what reason would Samantha have returned to them other than to bring them to safety?

To bring them some better life?

Mitts went about his duties. He, at least, was determined *not* to be distracted.

When he was quite certain nobody else was watching, he slipped out of the Village.

On his way out, he spotted Dag up on the rampart.

The two of them exchanged a salute.

He was pleased to see that at least one member of the Village hadn't lost all sense of routine.

Mitts headed down to the water's edge.

As he stood on the shore, he observed a pair of uniformed men standing on the boat.

They chatted casually to one another.

Mitts waved to them.

They waved back.

Mitts estimated the boat was just large enough for Samantha and the four men he'd so far counted. Anybody else and it would've been a real squeeze.

He trod along the water's edge.

He stared across the surface of the lake.

He tried to make out something on the other side.

But there was nothing to make out.

After a while, finished with his sleuthing, Mitts just stood and stared across the water.

He allowed himself to think.

A thousand random thoughts and feelings washed over him.

But he found himself caught on a single track:

She's back.

She's really back.

———

Mitts must've been standing at the water's edge for about half an hour before he heard the familiar voice behind him.

"At ease soldier."

He turned to look.

Samantha.

It was so strange.

She looked like she hadn't aged a day.

It was as if that fateful night had never happened.

She looked past Mitts. Out over the water. "Trying to work out where we came from?"

"Yeah," Mitts replied.

She extended a long, slender finger.

Pointed.

"You see that hillside, the one which dips down into a sort of V-shape?"

Mitts looked to where she pointed.

He had to admit that his vision wasn't the best.

Five years of night-time patrols hadn't helped.

"Well," Samantha continued, "if you follow the form of it downwards, about halfway to the water, you'll see."

Mitts squinted harder still.

He looked to where Samantha pointed.

The hillside.

The V-shape.

. . . And then he caught sight of it.

A dark object.

It might've been blue, or purple, or even green.

From here it was impossible to tell.

"What is it?" he said, turning back to her, breathing in a clean scent of lemon.

Wherever she'd come from there was, apparently, no end of scented soaps.

Samantha smiled. "You'll have to wait and see. If you come along, that is."

" 'Come along'?"

"You were on my shortlist, actually."

Mitts felt his heart give a gentle beat.

The blood rose all the way to the tips of his ears.

He stared back out over the water, as if it might prevent Samantha from seeing his reaction. "What about Luca?"

"Sure," Samantha replied. "She can come too—*every-body's* welcome."

Despite 'everybody being welcome', he noted the lack of enthusiasm in Samantha's tone when he mentioned Luca.

"What about Dag?"

"Dag . . . *Dag*," Samantha said, as if she was scouring her memory—as if she had forgotten who he was. "Well, if he really wants to, I don't see why not."

Several beats of silence followed.

Mitts felt himself itching from the inside.

There was still the unanswered mystery.

The one which nobody had thought prudent to ask after so far.

Mitts asked after it now.

Samantha remained quiet for a long few moments.

She stared into the distance.

Over the water. To the other side.

Maybe she was staring at the vehicle waiting there.

Waiting to take them away.

Finally, she explained. "It was just a . . . I don't know . . ." She averted his gaze, looked beyond him, back to the Village. "A silly plan, not even that, really. I saw an opportunity—an opportunity to finish with Dag. And, well, I . . . I decided to take it."

"Then it's true. You *did* shoot Dag?"

Samantha nodded.

She met his eye briefly then looked away.

"I thought it'd be the perfect cover," she said. "The mist was rolling in. The sound of gunfire all around." She shrugged. "Mistakes happen under those circumstances. Friendly fire."

"But he caught you," Mitts replied. "He saw what you were up to."

Samantha turned her hand over.

Gazed at her fingernails.

"I think I hit him in the leg. The ricochet caught his eye, too, I guess. And still he managed to grab my gun. To wrestle it off me." She smirked. "He's one wily customer, that Dag."

She looked back directly into Mitts's eyes.

The smirk disappeared.

Mitts felt a swirling sensation in his stomach.

It was one thing for her to be looking at him with those crystalline, blue eyes of hers.

Quite another for him to have imagined her *dead*.

. . . And yet, here she was, *re-animated*.

Standing before him.

"I told him to do it," she continued. "I told him to *shoot me* while he still could. With my own gun. But even though he had the opportunity, he didn't do it. He just shook his head. Told me to go." She jabbed her tongue hard into the side of her cheek. "I just did what he said." She pointed out into the water. "He told you I swam, didn't he? That I escaped by *swimming*?"

"Yes," Mitts replied, "we went out there, looking . . . but we couldn't find you. We only found your boots."

A long silence hung over the pair of them.

Mitts felt his chest tighten.

And then Samantha said, "Wanna know a secret—a tip that'll serve you well?"

"All right."

"Don't trudge about these hills in only your socks."

Mitts let out a laugh.

It sounded so unreal—so *alien*.

He almost choked on it.

———

On the way back through the Village gates, Mitts gazed upward.

To the rampart.

He caught sight of Dag again.

But this time Dag didn't acknowledge Mitts.

He appeared to be fixated on something in his hands. Perhaps one of the torches they used out on the Patrol. Although Dag no longer went out on Patrol, he remained a vital component; maintaining their gear, fixing things that, inevitably, got broken.

Mitts scolded himself for what he had thought following Samantha's disappearance.

How he had fooled himself that there was more to the story.

That *Dag* had been the one to take the opportunity to kill her.

As Mitts walked with Samantha through the Village, she asked about his life. About how things had been going. Mitts found it odd to reflect on how little had changed.

Nothing *visible*, in any case.

Nothing *Samantha* might've noticed.

He wasn't going to go into details of the fight he'd had with Luca that morning.

How she had finally turned him out onto the street.

Mitts asked after Samantha.

He wanted to know how she'd got involved with the armed men who'd shown up with her.

How they'd arrived by boat.

She told him about how she'd walked for days.

Trudging along the water's edge.

She had wanted to get the Village out of sight.

She explained how she had felt stifled. How she had felt that she could no longer live in the same place as Dag. That it would tear her apart if things went on the same way.

She needed to be in charge.

She went on to tell him that she had come across a dirt track.

She had followed it.

Wanting to see where it headed.

She told him how the hard, unruly ground had bruised her socked feet.

After a few hours, she had tossed her socks away. They'd become soaked in blood and sweat.

Walking barefoot, she told him, was easier than walking in socks.

Sometime later, she had heard an engine. Out in the darkness.

She had hidden from the sound.

Thrown herself into a ditch at the side of the track.

She had held herself still.

Sinking into the mud.

It was only when she heard car doors slamming directly above that she realised she had sunk into the mud up to her chest. And that she couldn't pull herself out.

She had no choice but to call out for help.

She went on to explain, in excruciating detail, how a pair of spotlights had blinked on.

How they had shone so brightly.

A pair of guards had helped her out of the ditch.

They had helped her into their truck.

Taken her away with them.

As they walked through the Village, many people came up to Samantha.

Some were happy, smiling at her.

Others clapped her on the shoulder. Glad to have her back.

More still clung to the edges of the street, not so much as wishing to cross paths with her.

Whether it was reverence, or fear, Mitts wasn't certain.

Perhaps a mixture of both.

Mitts pressed Samantha for further details on where she was living now.

But she remained coy.

All she would say was that he would 'see for himself' if he came with her.

Mitts noted—only too presciently—her tone of voice.

There was a subtle implication which suggested that—if Mitts *did* agree to come—the responsibility for the decision would be his and his alone.

Mitts didn't know how to feel about that.

So he made no response.

He refused to commit.

They approached the Station.

Samantha's escorts awaited her, chatting among themselves.

Their semi-automatics looked just as frightening simply hanging about their necks.

Both turned to Samantha, gave her a nod.

A slight smile.

As they trudged into the Station, Samantha soon found herself surrounded by her former companions, and she promised Mitts that they would speak later.

At that precise moment, the bomb went off.

The scientist brushes her red hair out of her lab coat collar.

She reaches across the glass capsule where—prostrate —-the creature lies.

Lifeless.

A chunk of matter.

Nothing more.

From a nearby shelf, she produces a clear vial, filled with a light-green liquid. She reaches past the vial to a disposable syringe. She shunts the syringe through the vial's seal.

She sucks the plunger upward, drawing out the light-green liquid.

That done, the measurement made, she replaces the vial on the shelf where it once was.

Then she turns her attention downward.

Onto the specimen.

She breathes in deeply. Her shoulders arch back.

The pulse in her throat beats hard.

She leans over the creature, then sinks the syringe into its body.

The light-green liquid disappears within its dark-purple veins.

So much like human veins.

She pulls back, drops the syringe into a metal bin.

She stares long and hard at the creature.

Waiting.

EVERYTHING CHANGED

The *ringing* in Mitts's ears was too much to bear.

He crunched his eyelids shut, trying to get shot of the noise in his head.

But it only made it worse.

He reached out about him.

Realised he was lying on the floor.

On the Station floor.

He could feel skin—*soft skin*.

He cracked an eyelid open.

Saw that it was Samantha.

She lay on her back.

Her chest rose and fell with troubled breathing.

Before Mitts knew it, he was up on his feet.

The world was a silent macabre spectacle.

Scattered bodies all around.

None of them moving.

No sound.

Mitts reached out. Took hold of Samantha's shoulders. He gave her a shake. He spoke to her.

But his voice never even reached his own ears.

He heard only ringing.

Burning . . . he could smell burning.

He breathed in.

Felt ash lining his throat.

He had to get out.

He had to get himself and Samantha out.

A muted crunching sound behind him.

Mitts turned to look.

A large beam which supported the ceiling.

Wilting beneath its own weight.

There was no time.

Soon it would collapse.

Mitts grabbed hold of Samantha's fingers. Entwined them with his own.

He dragged her toward the exit.

When he reached the doorway, he felt Samantha struggling against his hold.

He bent down to her. Spoke to her. Tried to get her to understand him.

But her eyes remained closed.

Her muscles resisted him.

He needed help.

He couldn't do this alone.

He released her. Trod away.

Outside, dust hung in the air.

Thick, grey clouds.

Everything flattened by the blast.

All he saw were bodies. Strewn through the streets.

The dainty, sallow plaster walls of the cottages crumbled.

They were covered in black dust.

When he looked down, he saw the faces of the two men who had escorted Samantha.

Their faces were peaceful.

Their eyes shut tight.

They continued to hold their rifles close to their chests.

Mitts walked on.

Several times, he stumbled.

But he kept himself upright.

He needed to get assistance . . . to save Samantha.

On his way out of the Village, Mitts felt a pang.

At the back of his head.

He turned his attention to a particular pile of rubble.

Déjà vu.

Familiar.

Yes, he had seen this before.

. . . Perhaps in a dream?

Mitts stood stock still. Hypnotised by the pile of rubble.

He stared long and hard.

Unable to believe.

There—beneath the rubble—he was *certain* he would find himself.

He crouched down.

Dug with his hands.

Brought one piece up.

Cast it away.

Another.

Then another.

Finally, he uncovered the person below.

Constantly rising black smoke dimmed the overcast daylight.

He removed another scrap.

Another.

And then he saw the face.

Her face.

Luca.

Her eyes lolled downward in their sockets.

Her lips were slightly parted.

Dusted with ash.

Lifeless.

The colour in her cheeks—*that glow*—was gone.

Replaced by a grey-purple colour.

The colour of *their* skin.

Mitts's breath shuddered out of him.

He stepped away.

She had been right.

Her dream had been right.

He broke into a run.

Headed out through the gates.

Away from the Village.

Away from the destruction.

As the ringing in his ears grew louder, he thought about his frustration this morning.

Hadn't he *wanted* to know what that dream had meant?

Well, now he did . . .

———

Outside the Village, Mitts faced off with one of Samantha's escorts.

Like the others, he bore a semi-automatic rifle.

Mitts stared into his eyes.

He sunk to his knees.

Held his hands up then clasped them behind his head.

In the near distance, Mitts made out another escort.

Ready to assist.

Mitts felt stabbing pains in his temples.

He closed his eyes.

The ringing in his ears was too much.

Something else put him on edge.

A second later, it struck him.

Sulphur.

It *stank* of sulphur.

These two escorts *absolutely stank* of sulphur.

Mitts tilted his head back.

He made eye contact with the escort who pointed his gun at him.

He stared hard into his eyes.

What did it mean?

The other escort got up close to Mitts.

He barked loudly in his ear.

He demanded to know where *she* was.

Mitts could hardly think to breathe.

Let alone talk.

He managed to tilt his head.

To mumble some reply.

To communicate that she was back in the Village.

That she was back *there*.

The escort with his gun pointed at Mitts, jerked him to his feet.

He led him in the direction of the water.

To the boat.

————

Mitts didn't sleep in the boat. But he struggled to recall any details of the journey.

Had they administered some drug?

They loaded him into a truck, on the other side of the water.

They placed a black hood over his head.

Mitts, still bleary from the constant ringing in his ears, asked them why this was necessary.

They told him that he 'hadn't yet committed'.

'Committed' to *what*?

But it didn't seem he was going to get answers any time soon.

They drove for what seemed like hours.

Mitts stirred from his daze. He heard a pair of slams.

The front doors of the truck being shut.

When they removed his hood, he saw it was dark.

The escorts helped him out of the truck.

Mitts rolled his shoulders. Tried to get himself shot of the aches from the journey.

His head felt sore.

Through narrowed eyes, he glanced out.

A garden.

Bristling. Full of life.

Sprawling green shoots. Brightly coloured flowers.

Chocolate-brown soil.

Lit up by an array of electric tea lights.

Almost like fairies.

The escorts led Mitts along the garden path.

Gravel crunched beneath his boots.

They passed by burbling streams, gurgling through guttering at their feet.

Mitts didn't feel afraid.

Should he?

He had lost everything.

Everything he cared about.

Everything he loved.

All over again.

He strained his neck to look back. To see where they had come from.

To see the truck.

The escort leading him forward shoved him in the back.

He jerked him around to face the direction they were travelling.

Deeper into the garden.

Mitts hadn't the strength to overpower the man.

Words came as a struggle. Squeezed out through dead-tired lips. ". . . Where is she? . . . Did you get her? . . . Is she still alive?"

Another shove in the back.

Before Mitts could ask again, the terrain beneath his feet changed.

The gravel was replaced by laminate flooring.

A pair of tinted glass doors appeared ahead.

"Where are we?" Mitts asked. "Where're we going?"

But the escort didn't respond.

———

The escort led Mitts along a series of corridors—corridors which reminded him of the Compound.

Mitts cast his mind back to those times in the middle of the night when he would stand up on that plastic box of his possessions, screwdriver in hand, and work at opening up the ventilation hatch.

There had been sheer excitement then.

An excitement which he hadn't been able to control.

He thought about dropping down through the ducts.

Into the forbidden areas of the Compound.

How he had trudged about the corridors, looking for something—*anything*—which might provide a distraction.

Any kind of distraction.

The escort thrust Mitts up six flights of stairs.

They arrived outside an unmarked door.

"Go in," the escort said.

Mitts eyed the semi-automatic which dangled over the escort's shoulder and did what he was told. Once he crossed the threshold, the door slammed shut behind him.

The room was almost entirely done out in white.

A window looked down on the garden outside.

In the distance, Mitts could make out rolling hills.

No sign of the lake.

He tried to open the window a little—to allow some air in—but it was sealed shut.

He tapped his fingernails against the windowpane. The plasticky sound told him it was reinforced glass. That any hope of escape would be in vain.

He would never break through.

Not without a wrecking ball.

There were twin beds. Each of them had white sheets. A fluffy, white towel sat neatly folded at the foot of each bed.

He explored further. Came across an en-suite bathroom.

No mirror. No shower curtain.

Nothing to put himself into any sort of danger.

No place to hide.

So this room was to be his new home.

For the time being.

His head still hummed from the explosion. But at least he could hear himself think.

Was that a good or bad thing?

Mitts slumped down in a white leather chair which sat by the window.

He propped his elbow on the armrest. Stared out at the garden.

There was nothing for him to do.

What seemed like half an hour later, there was an electric *buzz.*

A doorbell?

Mitts sat still, wondering what he was expected to do.

This *was* a prison cell, after all.

Wasn't it?

Were they going to bother with the pretence of privacy here?

Just as Doctor Heinmein had done back at the Compound...

Another *buzz*.

They really *were* insistent.

He shoved himself up and out of the chair.

"Come in," he muttered.

The door slid open.

Red hair.

White lab coat.

Slim posture.

She tilted her head to one side.

This couldn't be happening . . . it *couldn't* be happening . . . and yet, here she was.

The woman from his dreams.

———

"Carla," the red-headed scientist said, extending her hand to him.

Mitts stared long and hard at her well-manicured, delicate fingers. He decided someone might be watching this meeting, using it as some sort of measuring stick for his mental health.

He accepted her handshake.

She smelled lightly of mint.

"Mitts," he replied.

"Yes," Carla said, with a smile, the skin about her eyes crinkling, "I know."

She glanced about the bedroom, as if she was searching for something.

He noticed she wore a coral necklace. She constantly ran her fingertips across it.

She indicated the white leather chair. "Please," she said.

Mitts glanced to the door. It had already shut.

If he *did* get out the door then where would he run?

Mitts did as she said. He sunk into the chair. Feeling cramp setting in, he stretched his legs out.

In the truck, he'd had to fold his legs up in an uncomfortable fashion.

It felt good to have more space.

Carla perched on the edge of one of the neatly made beds.

Mitts's stomach grumbled.

Carla glanced to him, that same smile clinging to her lips. "Hungry?" she said.

"A little," Mitts admitted.

"Don't worry. We'll bring in something for you to eat— just a few questions first, that's all."

Mitts expected Carla to dig out a computer tablet, or, at the very least, a paper notepad and pencil.

He supposed the hidden cameras, surely dotted around the room, would be quite sufficient for keeping a record of this meeting.

Carla stuffed her hands into the pockets of her lab coat. She leaned back a little on the bed, making the mattress springs creak. "So, *Mitts*," she said, putting extra stress on his name. "Tell me about the dreams."

Mitts felt a chill pass through his gut.

He glanced at her briefly, almost unable to understand the invitation.

Then his mind came to a conclusion:

Samantha.

Of course.

She had told them.

About these *prophetic* dreams of his.

Was that the reason why Samantha had wanted him to come here with her?

Mitts fixed Carla with a stare. It was deeply unnerving to be sitting here with this woman who'd been present in his dreams. "Why don't you tell me what went on?" he said. "What caused the explosion back at the Village?"

When Mitts heard his voice coming back at him, he was surprised at how insistent he sounded.

And a little impressed with himself.

He had managed to hold his resolve.

Carla exhaled daintily. "Please, Mitts, it's important we hear about your dreams." She widened her eyes. "You've seen me, haven't you? You've seen me in the dreams you've been having lately?"

Mitts felt his chest tighten.

His stomach dipped.

He glanced about the room. He felt restless.

He stood.

Paced back and forth.

Mitts imagined those watching would see this as an act of aggression. That it was all they would need to pounce. He expected the door to burst open. For those escorts to come busting in.

Ready to gun him down.

But nobody came.

And Carla didn't so much as flinch.

Mitts stared long and hard at her.

He bunched his fingers into fists.

"The dreams?" he said.

"Yes, Mitts," Carla replied. "The *dreams*."

Mitts paused his pacing.

He stared out the window.

Down to the garden below.

To the flickering tea lights.

He allowed himself a wry smile.

"The whole world is tumbling down and you think about an ornamental garden?"

When he looked back at Carla, she gave him a neutral smile.

Mitts shook his head. "Where'd those creatures come from, huh? Is it *you*? Have you been manufacturing them here? Are they *human* creations?"

Like before, Carla made no response.

Just that same, neutral smile.

Tell us about the dreams, Mitts, he imagined her saying.

Mitts breathed in deeply.

He glanced around the room. "Ever since I came here," Mitts said, "I started to have dreams . . . strange, vivid—*lucid* —dreams."

He looked to Carla.

She fed him a nod of encouragement.

"First," Mitts continued, "dreams about dancers. On a balcony. New Year's Eve." He shook his head. "It came back, again and again . . ."

"How long ago was this, Mitts?" Carla said, breaking her silence.

Mitts shook his head. He gazed out the window.

It was pitch black outside now.

The glow of the garden below seemed almost other-worldly.

Ethereal.

"I was eleven when we left home, when I left home with my family, and then—"

Something caught in his throat.

"We know what happened, Mitts, and you must realise that we're *very* sorry." She paused for a moment as if to indi-cate the emotional weight which her voice *didn't* carry. "What concerns us is the *dreams*—we need to know about the *dreams*."

"Right," Mitts said, pressing his forehead up against the cool windowpane. "The dreams."

———

Again, Mitts had no way of knowing how much time really passed.

There was no clock.

Only the night moving by outside the window.

His brain kept buzzing.

He told Carla everything she needed to know about his dreams.

As much as he was able to recall after all these years.

When he reached the end, when he had told Carla about his latest dreams—the ones which'd featured *her*—he restrained the urge to ask straight out how they had done it.

How they had invaded his mind.

Instead, he turned his mind to another matter.

"There was another person," Mitts said. "Back in the Village."

Carla rose up from the bed, on her way out.

Apparently she'd got everything she needed.

"Yes," she replied. "Luca."

It felt as if someone had slipped a knife into Mitts's stomach.

He had hardly made sense of all that had happened. Those words Luca had spoken. How she had told him to 'Get out'. That he was welcome no longer . . . and then she had *died*.

Just like that.

Simple as a *click* of the fingers.

"It didn't really matter which one of you came," Carla went on. "We just needed one for the purposes of our studies."

Suddenly, Mitts felt an inexplicable rage dawn on him.

He turned on Carla.

A snarl took hold of his mouth.

"Get out."

Carla held still. She showed no fear.

This only enraged Mitts all the more.

"*Get out!*" he repeated, louder.

Again, not so much as a flinch from Carla.

She tilted her head to one side.

Affecting some kind of *sympathetic* façade.

As she left, Mitts felt the anger humming through him.

Throttling his blood.

He swallowed the knot out of his throat.

Found the strength to raise his voice one more time.

"You're watching me here, aren't you?" He glared about the room. "What is it? Cameras? Sound? What're you watching me with, huh?"

Carla remained at the door.

The door, slow and steady, slid open.

Carla glanced to Mitts, then tapped her temple with a self-satisfied smile.

She left him alone.

All alone.

———

After Carla had left, an escort entered. He served Mitts dinner on a plastic tray. The cutlery, too, was plastic. The escort stood over him as he ate, watching each and every one of his gestures with great care. As if any one might be the killing stroke.

One thing was for certain, if Mitts *did* attempt to slash his throat with the plastic knife provided, it would take hours.

Once he had finished up dinner—a damp quiche accompanied by some over-boiled vegetables—he lay back on one of the beds, staring at the ceiling.

He remained like that until the sun rose.

Until its rays beamed in through the window.

Although he was weary, and would've liked nothing more than to drift off to sleep, the thought of having Carla back inside his unconscious mind prevented him from so much as closing his eyes.

What did they want him for?

How had they known about the dreams?

How had they known about *Luca* having the same dreams?

Outside, Mitts heard a truck pull up.

He didn't get up.

If they wished to keep him here—like some *zoo animal*—then he would make sure he was as *uninteresting* as possible.

As *unhelpful* as he could manage.

They could take nothing from him now.

Only his life.

And he wasn't even really sure he had *that* any longer.

A little while later, Mitts heard the door slide open again.

Even the simple reaction of getting to his feet seemed like a minor defeat.

He wanted nothing short of a total mental shutdown.

He wanted to *ruin* their experiments . . . whatever they were.

Mitts examined the pair of figures in the doorway.

A man and a woman.

Both wore the escorts' uniform.

The woman—Mitts realised—was Samantha.

Samantha turned to the escort. She insisted that she be alone with Mitts.

After a brief hesitation, the escort relented.

The door shut on him.

Leaving him outside.

For a long few moments, feeling sleep almost overcoming him now, Mitts regarded Samantha.

Her blond hair.

Her blue eyes.

How she wore the same navy-blue uniform as *them*.

He thought about how she had tricked them all.

Made them all think her dead.

While she had been alive.

Samantha gave Mitts a faint smile.

He didn't smile back.

He eyed the bruise on her forehead, but said nothing about it.

"We're the only survivors," Samantha said. "Aside from the two escorts. The ones down by the water's edge—the ones who captured you." She paused for a moment, looked Mitts hard in the eye. "What'd you think about that?"

"Who set off the bomb?"

Samantha gave a slight shrug. A vague pout. Then she looked out the window.

To the dawning day outside.

"Dag."

"*Dag?*" Mitts said, almost choking his name out. "But . . . *why?*"

"Because," Samantha replied, "he always thought that I was going to come back. He had to have some sort of counterattacking measure."

Mitts shook his head. "I don't understand . . ."

"Dag knew a lot more than what he let on, Mitts. He knew all about this place—all about *these* people. He knew that, when he let me go, I would most likely end up in their clutches." She smiled faintly. "And so it turned out. He obviously felt that there was a good possibility I would come back. He couldn't handle the idea of losing control of the Village; the control which he had won at last."

"If you knew about the bomb why didn't you do something to prevent it?"

Samantha shook her head. "I knew nothing about the bomb. Nothing about what Dag had planned, really. But there was something we needed from the Village."

"Me?"

Samantha tilted her head to one side.

Broke off his gaze.

"Or Luca."

She breathed in deeply.

Mitts observed how her cheeks puffed up.

How the gesture seemed to make her eyes bulge out of their sockets.

It almost made her ugly.

"We tried our best to be subtle about it," Samantha continued. "The original plan was for us to sneak into the Village at night. It seemed a good enough bet that we would miss the Patrol for the evening. But we weren't lucky." She shrugged. "There was no way for us to avoid it happening the way it did . . . if Dag had only been more patient, waited for us to extract you, or Luca, then we would've been gone. Never to return."

Mitts allowed himself to fume for several moments.

He didn't want to lash out.

It would only serve to make a mockery of himself.

Show that he could be easily provoked.

"Why didn't he say anything?" Mitts finally got out.

"I don't know. He was the only one who *could've* known, unless he confided in someone else"—her voice brightened a touch as she looked to Mitts, something which ill-suited the mood of the room—"but, hey, Dag confiding in somebody else, doesn't sound at all likely, now, does it?"

Mitts looked to Samantha again. "Why were we the only survivors?"

"There's such a thing as fate."

"I don't believe you. There's something else, isn't there? Something you're not telling me."

"Listen, Mitts, I think you've got an overinflated sense of my worth here. About my role at the Facility. Do you think I *really* know what's going on? Or do you think they used me as a usefully placed device to get what they wanted? Huh? What'd you think?"

Mitts stayed quiet for a long while. "I don't know what to think," he said, finally.

He expected Samantha to leave once their talking fell away, but, on the contrary, she remained in the room. She lay down on the other bed. Rested her hands across her stomach and stared at the ceiling. After a while, she turned to him. "You can sleep if you like. It'll make all this much easier to process."

Mitts sent her a gnarled smile back. "It *would* make it easier, wouldn't it?"

"You're worried about them going digging in your mind while you sleep."

Mitts stayed quiet.

"I'll stay here, with you," she said. "Until you wake up."

Mitts felt his eyelids drooping.

And he realised he no longer had the energy to resist.

────────

It had been so long since Mitts had experienced a dreamless sleep that he could hardly believe he had slept at all. He opened his eyes, glanced to his side, and saw Samantha lying there.

She was watching him. A slight smile on her lips.

"You were out for a good fourteen hours," she said.

Sure enough, when Mitts looked out the window, he saw that the sun was on its way back down.

Night, once more, was draping itself over the landscape.

Samantha reached up to her face. Her fingers stroked the three neat scars she had there.

The ones which Mitts had noticed the first time they'd met.

"I want to tell you about my scars," she said. "Would you listen?"

"Don't think I've got much choice—isn't this the definition of a 'captive audience'?"

Samantha smiled back at him. "I think it'll help to explain —explain the reason *why* me and Dag felt so strongly set against one another."

Mitts held himself still.

He could feel his heart pounding hard in his cheeks.

At his throat.

He already believed he'd put together some of the pieces.

But, when he'd brought up her scars before, she'd batted him away.

"Will you listen?" she said.

"Yes," Mitts replied, his dry throat coming out in his voice.

"I used to work as a waitress," she said. "*Before*—I worked in this tiny little town, its name doesn't matter. I rented a room above a pub in exchange for doing the cleaning up in the mornings . . . mopping up puked-over floors, polishing up the bar counter, you know, that sort of thing."

Mitts felt his heart flutter up to his chest.

He thought about their age difference.

He had only been eleven when he had left home.

Samantha had to have been at least five years older.

Now that he was twenty-three did that make her twenty-eight?

Older?

She continued. "I always wanted to be a singer, I had a guitar and a little notebook where I'd scribble down the lyrics." She released a sigh, one which sounded as if it'd been sustained for an *awfully* long time. "My dream was to play concerts, to play in front of a crowd. But *that* was never going to happen. I was paralysed by nerves doing anything *at all* in public, and sometimes when I worked waitressing, my voice would wobble; I'd feel the strain of those eyes all watching me."

Mitts thought about how he had never—not for one *second*—seen Samantha as anything other than one-hundred-per-cent confident.

She was a *leader*.

A *born* leader.

"I suppose I was in a rut," she continued. "I didn't quite want to admit the dream hadn't worked out, and that I should go try something else with my life, and maybe—given five, six months—I would've figured it out for myself . . . but then everything *stopped*."

Mitts surveyed Samantha's face. The fine cut of her jawbone. How her blond hair draped down.

He supposed, on another girl, her hair might've softened the outline of her face.

But not with Samantha.

If anything it made her face *sharper*.

More *dangerous*.

Everything about Samantha's aspect screamed to him that he should take care.

That she always had something up her sleeve.

Samantha went on. "I remember seeing the news on TV —I'd been at work at the time. I was just taking my apron off over my blouse. Our last clients for the evening had just left the premises without paying. Just rushed up and left. Outside, I heard the *squeal* of tyres. At first, I thought that it was the customers, trying to make a fast getaway. To see if they could survive."

Here her throat seemed to constrict.

The words seemed to get lost for a few moments.

"If they could *escape* the rain."

Mitts turned his mind back to his own memories of the rain.

To it drumming down on the roof of Heinmein's car.

And to the general sense of panic which'd clung to its presence.

Samantha looked down over herself.

At the navy-blue uniform—*their uniform*—which she wore.

"Outside, there was a car beeping its horn. I slipped out through the door of the restaurant, and, I don't know . . . I really don't know what possessed me; I was already so used to nuisance old men, the ones who'd honk at me in the street, and I knew never to pay them any attention. But, in the end, I approached the open window. I peered inside."

"Who was it?"

"Dag . . . and someone else."

Mitts decided not to push to know the 'someone else'.

"They told me they had somewhere to go, that they had a safe place where we could all ride out the rising tides, where we could all *survive*." Here, Samantha rolled her eyes. "And I suppose I was stupid enough to fall for that one." She shook her head slightly. "Though I guess that if a girl's ever going to

STRANGERS IN THE NIGHT

make a fool out of herself then it's going to be when the apoc-alypse is in town, huh?"

"Yeah," Mitts said, with a smile. "I guess so."

"They drove on through the night, and I remember telling them, over and over again, that they were going the wrong way. It seemed that the entirety of the other traffic on the road was headed in the exact opposite direction to us. But Dag, he kept on reassuring me. And so I trusted them. I sat slumped up in the back seat. Fell asleep."

Mitts closed his eyes a moment. He massaged his eyelids with his fingertips.

Everything felt tight and tired.

"There were others, too," Samantha continued, "on the way there Dag was shouting for people to join us. Lots of them did. About ten, fifteen cars, in all . . . the others who came to live in the Village." She paused for a moment. "I don't know precisely *when* it happened, but I remember the rain drumming against the roof—it hammering down on us —and the car driving uphill *all* the time. I could feel the nausea of taking all those bends on the mountain roads. Kept feeling my stomach shrinking back down. But when it seemed like we'd been climbing up those roads for hours and hours, we came to a sudden stop. Dag got out of the car, all in a hurry. He banged on my window, told me that I had to get out too. When I did get out, I found we were parked up in a layby, and that, up ahead, there was this large truck—the kind that somebody might use for transporting cattle. He told us we all needed to get in the back. Dag . . ."

"And the other guy," Mitts put in, without thinking.

Samantha met Mitts with a smouldering glare.

He regretted having said anything at all.

"Dag, and the *other* guy, got into the truck cab. The rest of us piled on into the back, under the tarpaulin. All of us sitting on the floor, the soles of our feet touching those of the person opposite. There was an awful racket about people wanting to bring their stuff with them and we lost quite a few who wouldn't leave their cars behind—let alone the *stuff* in their cars. They just drove off, back in the direction we came. They couldn't be helped."

Mitts felt a pang in his chest.

"Then what happened?" he said.

Samantha shrugged. "I dunno, it all got dark from there, and nobody could manage to open the back doors of the truck. We were trapped."

———

Samantha's story was interrupted by a *buzz* at the door.

Mitts sat upright. He dangled his feet off the edge of the bed.

He was feeling a little better now.

His mind was a little clearer.

Less *cluttered* . . . if that was at all possible.

As if—*finally*—he was getting some truth about the situation.

All it had taken was the death of everybody he had known and loved . . .

When Samantha called out for the person at the door to come in, one of the escorts was there, bearing a pair of plastic trays this time.

A dollop of steaming white rice. A chicken leg alongside it.

Mitts thought to himself that this might be the perfect time to take the escort off guard.

His hands were full.

He wouldn't be able to easily grab his semi-automatic.

The escort snapped around.

He *glared* at Mitts.

And Mitts saw the wire which snaked up to his ear.

Someone had tipped him off.

Someone had read Mitts's mind.

Before Mitts could react, the escort dropped the tray.

Food splattered all across the floor.

Samantha screamed.

The escort shoved Mitts onto his back. Onto the bed.

He shoved his rifle into the underside of Mitts's chin.

Every muscle in Mitts's body drew tight.

He gritted his teeth.

Before Mitts had really got his head around what'd gone on, the escort backed off.

For a few seconds, Mitts's heart beat loudly in his ears.

His whole body numbed.

When he reached up to his mouth, his fingertips came away with a thin layer of blood.

He glanced up.

His vision blurred.

He saw the escort.

Samantha . . . she was gripping the escort's arm.

Yanking him away from Mitts.

The escort's eyes never left Mitts.

His hold on his rifle never let up.

Not for a second.

Mitts realised the escort now pointed his rifle to the ceiling. That Samantha was talking sense into him. Mitts propped himself up onto his side, using his elbow.

He made the conscious decision not to think about anything.

He fixed his thoughts on the white-washed walls.

That seemed to do the trick.

Finally, Samantha managed to cajole the escort into leaving the room. She told him that she would clean up the mess on the floor. She told him to go and fetch a second helping.

Truth be told, Mitts had lost his appetite.

When the escort was gone, Samantha used wadded-up toilet paper to clean the mess.

Mitts felt himself shaking.

He was still in shock.

"What the *hell* just happened?" he said.

Samantha paused her cleaning. She gripped the fistful of soiled toilet paper tightly.

Fixed Mitts with a glare.

"What do you *think* happened?"

"They're monitoring my thoughts, aren't they?" Mitts felt a lump form in his throat. "There're no cameras in here, the place isn't even wired for sound, is it? All they need to do is *see* what I'm thinking . . . that's the greatest surveillance they could ever ask for."

Samantha didn't respond.

Anger flashed through him.

"That's it, *isn't it?*"

Samantha held his gaze.

"That's why they brought you here, Mitts," Samantha replied. "I thought it had been made clear that your *mind* is what they're after. They're not going to risk losing you—not going to risk any damage coming to you."

"Funny, I'm pretty convinced that a guy just shoved a gun in my face. Seems a strange place to want to shoot someone whose brain is so important, huh?"

Samantha stared back at him. Stone-faced.

Then she gave a smirk.

She turned her attention back downward. To the clean-up job.

"Glad you've still got your sense of humour," she said.

"Yeah," Mitts said, staring out the window to the approaching night. "I guess I still have *something*."

————————

Their second dinner arrived. Mitts ate nothing.

He pushed his rice and chicken about his plate with his plastic fork.

This situation reminded him of those Sunday evenings in the Restricted Area. He would lose his appetite then, too. It was the knowledge that, later, Heinmein would put each of them through their check-up. That he would have to submit to the *scientist's* will.

There was no table in the room, so they ate their dinner perched on the edge of the bed.

When Mitts glanced up, he saw Samantha had almost finished her dinner.

She only had a few scraps of rice left.

She had no reason *not* to have an appetite.

This was just a normal day at the office for her.

The Facility was her *home* now, after all.

Samantha looked to him, then to his plate.

With a slight smile twisting her lips, she rose up off the edge of the bed.

She took his plate off him—still more than three-quarters full.

She left the plates by the door.

Then she returned to the bed.

The two of them sat on the edge of the mattress.

"So," she said. "Want to hear the end of the story?"

Mitts felt a resistance grow within him.

More than anything else, he wanted to tell her no.

He wanted to see the look on her face when he told her that he *didn't* want to hear what had happened to her.

How she had come to arrive at the Village.

But then curiosity got the better of him.

He told her to continue.

And she did.

She told him how they travelled through the night in the back of the truck.

How movement had been more or less constant.

Several of Samantha's fellow passengers had suffered from travel sickness. No matter how hard they bashed their fists up against the cab, there was no reaction from either of the drivers.

With a shake of her head, she told Mitts how they had arrived at the tiny village.

At what would be their home for the foreseeable future.

There were animals running free about the place.

It seemed there had been a farm there once.

They set about *making* the place their home.

Bringing *life* to the Village.

It was there that Samantha stopped.

Mitts felt his whole body surging with adrenalin—hunger

too?—wanting to hear what was coming next. "You didn't tell me how you got the scars," he said.

Samantha met his eyes, unsmiling. "The other man—the one who travelled with Dag," she said, her voice catching in her throat.

For a long second, Mitts was certain Samantha would burst into tears.

Mitts planned on being cold.

If she wanted a shoulder to cry on she could go fetch one of those escorts.

Samantha held herself back.

Just like she *always* did.

"His name was Jake, but everyone used to call him 'Jay'," she said, "and, well, as time went on, there was a *thing* between us."

"A 'thing'?" Mitts repeated back at her, more struck by the descent into schoolyard language than the implied meaning.

Samantha just nodded. "Yes, we got close." She drew in a deep breath. Her chest puffed out. She gripped the edge of the mattress so tightly that her knuckles turned white. "He and Dag, they were the only ones—the only ones who knew where we were . . . they'd . . . they'd brought us to the Village." She sniffed a laugh through her nose. "For some reason, at the beginning, I thought I'd get close to Jake. See if I couldn't get some more information on our situation out of him. But he gave nothing away. He seemed to be wary of tricks. And I ended up *loving* him."

Mitts felt his gut turn in a knot.

He tasted the little of the chicken and rice he had forced down.

He felt obscenely hot for a moment, and then cold.

Feeling a pounding sensation at his temples, he reached up.

As if some invisible force was attempting to rap its knuckles against his skull.

Samantha went on. "There were power games between Jake and Dag—there always were. It was inevitable that things would come to blows eventually." She shook her head, apparently out of disbelief. "It was out there, at the water's edge." She gave a slight smile. "Strange how everything always seemed to happen out there . . . the two of them just started laying into one another; exchanging blows. Only when I got in the middle of them did I realise Dag had a knife."

She turned full on to Mitts.

Drew so close that he could feel the warmth from her breath.

Mitts stared at the red-raw, half-healed trio of scars.

In the too-bright light of the room, the skin gave off a greyish reflection.

He thought about reaching out to touch the scars.

Was that what she wanted?

On impulse, he twisted his neck around. To get a look at Samantha's ears.

Nothing.

No earbud.

When he turned his attention back onto Samantha's blue, blue eyes, she was smiling again.

"Don't worry," she said. "I like life's mysteries—I don't need to see your brain."

He held her gaze. Their lips were only centimetres apart. "What do they want from me?"

"Just your cooperation," Samantha said, leaning in closer still.

"My 'cooperation'?"

Her mouth moved onto his.

Mitts felt as though his blood had caught fire.

His heart beat harder and harder.

They kissed.

When Samantha drew back, her eyes still on his, she said, "Is that too much to ask?"

The red-haired scientist—CARLA—holds her hand to the creature's chest.

Her pale, white fingers fan out.

She waits for a pulse.

Any sign of life.

But the eyes remain black.

No sign of consciousness.

Not yet.

But the scientist remains unperturbed. Her hand remains on the chest. Insistent that she shall get what she wishes for. That much is certain.

When she leans back again—takes in the creature once more—a tiny, little light appears within those black eyes.

The scientist takes a couple of steps back.

Smiles.

ANOTHER LIFE, ANOTHER START

Mitts sat on a carved stone seat in the garden which stood at the front of the Facility.

He listened to the gargle of the water through guttering.

One of the escorts had just been by to water the plants. And the gutters were carrying the excess away.

When Mitts breathed in, all he could smell was soil.

A rich, full taste.

It reminded him of the Village.

He could never quite get over the scents of nature.

He could never quite forget those seven long years of sensory deprivation down in the Restricted Area. And what had happened after . . .

Life was good at the Facility. Or as good as it ever had been.

They took good care of him.

He had given them his full cooperation.

The Facility had assigned him a therapist:

A woman in her fifties called Lilly.

At first Mitts was extremely wary about telling Lilly *anything*. He had to admit he feared the therapy sessions were some sort of elaborate device—a device for the Facility administration to check just how honest he was being.

But the truth was, Mitts had no energy left to resist.

He had nowhere to go.

The warm sunshine beamed down upon him. He thought about all that had happened since he had 'cooperated'. Those in charge had explained things to him. They had informed him that the 'Village' had always been intended as a sort of proving ground. A means for the Facility to release its stock of creatures upon a human population.

And examine the results.

Dag and Jake had been lower-level employees.

Charged with the task of recruiting as many desperate —*fleeing*—human beings as they could.

To begin with, the Facility had merely observed the creatures' reaction to humans.

But, as Carla—the red-haired scientist—had confided in him, it had become clear that the more interesting branch of the experiment had turned out to be the humans' reaction to the creatures.

Carla informed Mitts that, most nights, they would

release their stock of creatures upon the Village. Then sit back and watch the results.

When the rains had first started to fall, the creatures had appeared.

Roaming all over the planet. Morbidly obese. Human-sized slugs.

At least that was how Carla had described them . . .

Indeed, their colloquial name around the Facility was 'Slugs'.

In more polite company, their name shifted to 'Strangers'.

The Facility had got hold of a specimen early on. And they had cloned the creature.

Carla told Mitts all the observations they'd made of the Strangers.

How they appeared to have an aversion to dry land.

And a love of water.

It was believed, Carla told him, that the creatures were directly linked to the apocalypse.

They had materialised with the falling rain.

With the surging floods.

The water which'd consumed the larger part of the world.

Although there was no evidence, it was supposed that the creatures had brought these waters along with them. From *wherever* they had come from:

Another dimension?

It was a lot of information for Mitts to absorb.

Mitts grew to despair Carla's smirks.

As if she revelled in his confusion.

In him getting to grips with such basics.

The Facility had contact with several other research centres scattered about the globe.

They were few and far between.

Transport—at present—was impossible.

There was just no way to span the great distances.

They relied on satellite communication.

Matching up data; comparing information.

Drawing conclusions.

But, as far as Mitts could tell from his time at the Facility, there were—*really*—no definite conclusions to draw.

Finally, when he plucked up the courage, he asked after his family.

If the Facility had known about Doctor Heinmein.

Carla had to clear permission to share such details. She got the go-ahead from her superior.

She informed Mitts that his family had been delivered to the Compound under the orders of the Facility.

Theirs, though, had been a different programme.

One which had been set for a ten-year observation period.

They never got past Year Seven.

Mitts had made sure of that.

Carla even showed Mitts graphs.

Charts drawn up as a result of the studies.

From the *data* Heinmein had fed back to the Facility.

"When you grew ill," Carla told him, one day, in one of

the top-floor laboratories, "we had Heinmein give you a dose of serum—*untested*. It was taken from the Strangers. We've found, in our experience, that their blood has certain *healing* properties in humans."

"Heinmein told me I would die in a week."

Carla nodded. "That happened in all the other cases." She smiled gently. "But the batch administered to you seemed to get the balance just right."

Mitts kept his thoughts to himself.

About how he had snuck through the air vents.

Come into contact with one of the Strangers.

How he believed *that* had been the factor which'd led to his healing.

In fact, he *hoped* that would be the case.

He didn't want to feel thankful to the Facility for anything.

He didn't want to feel thankful to *Heinmein* for anything.

Often, when Mitts glanced at Carla, he observed a faraway look in her eyes. He believed it to be a signal to whoever was watching them.

That they should be ready.

On standby.

Weapon drawn.

He also asked Carla why the Facility hadn't stepped in to save his parents.

Carla looked away then.

As if ashamed.

She mumbled something about Heinmein having lost his mind.

An 'unanticipated' variable.

Mitts had held himself back.

But only just.

Because he knew the truth.

Even if Carla wouldn't spoon feed him that particular morsel.

In the Facility, someone—*somewhere*—had surely taken the executive decision that it would make an interesting 'experiment' to observe Mitts's attempts to integrate with the Village.

They had known beforehand—*somehow*—that Mitts possessed the same 'Gift' as Luca.

Carla claimed this phenomenon was present in one in a thousand.

Or so said their data.

They had wanted to observe how those who possessed the Gift reacted in group situations.

How they functioned with a community surrounding them.

At the end of their conversations, he asked Carla if what Samantha had told him had been a lie.

If it had indeed been Dag who had placed the explosives.

But Carla only pressed her lips together. Shook her head. "No, he really *did* hate us—all of *you*. He wanted to burn down everything. Finish it off."

Mitts shook his head, almost unable to absorb the idea.

But, he supposed, it might not be the truth.

Why should they tell him the truth when he would take a lie just as easily?

Mitts pressed his back up against the stone seat in the garden.

He could hear the *hum* of an engine closing on him.

The *crunch* of gravel passing beneath the heavy weight of approaching tyres.

He bent his head back. Stared long and hard at the soaring blue sky.

The neat, bright blur which was the sun.

Some days he thought about running away.

Some days he thought about *finishing* it all.

He looked to the truck as it pulled up.

Its tyres locked.

They slid along the loose gravel.

A series of escorts, all dressed in navy-blue uniforms, stepped out.

An elderly man emerged between them.

He was stick thin.

Dressed in a pin-striped suit.

He wore a cravat with a silver pin.

One of the escorts helped support his weight.

The man looked frail. *So* frail.

It was hard to believe this was him.

The man who would peer into his mind.

———

Mitts lay down on the examination table.

He heard the paper sheet beneath him crumple.

The air smelled strongly of disinfectant.

Mitts hadn't had a sense of this level of *clinical* cleanliness since he had been a young boy.

He'd fallen over. Scraped his knee . . . only it wasn't a normal scrape.

The blood had just kept on flowing.

He'd required stitches.

His parents had taken him down to the local doctor's surgery.

A GP had swabbed his cut.

That swab smelled like the air here.

There was something about *disinfectant* which made the hairs stand up at the back of his neck.

A substance specifically existing to neutralise something invisible to the naked eye.

Something which might not even be there.

Mitts glanced about.

His feet stuck up at the end of the table.

The floor beneath him was all laminate tiling.

It reminded him of the flooring back at the Compound.

He looked to the elderly man. The scientist who'd arrived from the other end of the country . . . what had *been* the country.

A *special* visitor.

The elderly man had a poor bedside manner.

With the help of a deferent escort, he shrugged a lab coat on over his shoulders.

Next, he tapped away at a touchscreen.

The gateway to a large bank of hard discs; computers.

Whatever it was.

The escort remained standing in the doorway.

Mitts tried to get a look at the touchscreen display. He could make nothing of the constantly moving charts. The numbers which flickered up and down the screen.

The elderly man jabbered in a low, gnarled-up voice to an assistant—a much younger man who had arrived with him.

The assistant, also in a lab coat, had frosty blond hair and a beer gut.

He worked quickly, smiling pleasantly at Mitts as he adjusted the wires and suckers arranged about his forehead and scalp.

Mitts didn't feel like a patient.

He felt more like an audience member.

A *passenger*.

Soon enough, the equipment was in place.

The elderly man stood over the bank of computers. His fingers flipped over the touchscreen.

Precision which belay his otherwise frail demeanour.

He occasionally muttered to his assistant, but, mostly, he muttered to himself.

Mitts sensed the growing unease in the room as he observed the scientists at work.

As he lay there, on the examination table, he was dimly aware of another presence.

Of *something else*.

He attempted to look around.

"Stay still, please," the elderly scientist scolded.

Mitts obeyed.

The elderly scientist made some minor adjustment to the suckers on his scalp.

"Doctor Smith?" the blond assistant said.

The elderly scientist—'Doctor Smith', apparently—crossed the room.

Mitts took the opportunity to get a better look at his surroundings.

The room was tight.

Clearly kept off to some nook or cranny of the Facility.

Whatever went on in this room, they didn't want anybody stumbling upon it.

Then again, most of what went on about the Facility, wasn't supposed to be stumbled upon.

He closed his eyes.

What he could hear—what he could *feel*—was a sort of low-level crackling.

Almost like static inside his own head.

It was like a night when he had woken from a nightmare.

It had been thundering outside.

He had shifted out of bed. Gone downstairs.

He had opened the back door. Stood in the rain for several minutes.

He could still recall the soaking sensation of the rain up against his skin.

Plastering his boxer shorts.

Smearing his hair to his forehead.

But it had been that *chatter* in the air which'd drawn his attention.

A radio tuned between stations.

A TV spewing white noise.

Something there . . . and yet *not*.

"Mr Thornestone?"

Mitts glanced up.

Until now, nobody involved with the Facility had admitted to knowing his surname.

He hadn't heard it in a long time.

Not since he had been back in school.

Doctor Smith met his eye. He gave him a slender smile.

Did Doctor Smith have one of those earpieces snaking up his neck?

Was there someone in a darkened room informing him exactly what Mitts was thinking?

"Would you like to know," Doctor Smith said, in his reedy, seemingly *weakening* voice, "how exactly it is that we can read your thoughts?"

Mitts had no idea how to respond.

Doctor Smith turned his back.

He looked to his blond assistant.

He gave him a firm nod.

The assistant flipped a switch on the wall.

Mitts expected it to be a light switch.

He thought that the whole room would suddenly be bathed in fierce white light.

In the distance, across the room, something illuminated.

Mitts strained his eyes.

He saw, in actual fact, that it was another room.

Adjacent to this one.

Identical in every way.

Divided by a two-way mirror.

He absorbed the sight beyond the glass.

One of those creatures.

One of the *Strangers*.

Like him, it was hooked up to a whole host of wires.

Propped up on an examination table.

Mirror images.

And yet they were destined to be bound together.

When Mitts's eyes opened he wasn't in the real world any longer.

He *was* apart *from it.*

No longer was he lying down . . . he was standing up.

Sulphur . . . in his nostrils, down his throat . . . in his lungs.

When he peered about, he realised he stood on a water-like substance.

It reminded him of the lake.

He stretched his mind back to those times when the creatures had come.

All of them hovering over the surface of the water.

He stretched his mind further.

Tried to work out how it might be possible.

And he came up with . . . nothing at all.

The air was a light-grey tone.

An overcast day.

And yet, different from any overcast day Mitts had experienced.

The air had a mystical quality to it.

A buzzing layer of static.

Invisible, and yet, when he reached out, he could feel it.

He thought of bumblebees. Crawling up and down his arms.

He knew he should panic.

But—strangely—he felt at peace with himself.

As if he might never have worries again.

Never in his life.

He gazed across the water.

Terrain sprouted up.

Dark-purple land masses.

Hills.

He could hardly believe it.

It was just like his dream . . . and yet this was a dream.

He only needed someone to wake him . . .

...U*P!*"

Mitts came to right away.

He felt as if his skin was melting.

As if the air itself was too hot.

"Come on now. *Wake up*, Mr Thornestone. *Wake up!*"

The voice was calm. Yet insistent.

Doctor Smith's voice.

Mitts propped himself up on his elbows.

He felt a cool hand across his forehead.

"That's it, that's it."

The tones of Doctor Smith's voice were calming.

"Good boy," Doctor Smith said. "You're coming round now."

Mitts allowed Doctor Smith to ease him back down flat.

Onto the examination table.

Mitts rested his head back on a too-thin pillow.

He blinked once—*twice*.

He tried to clear his eyes.

Clear his eyes of the landscape he had just seen.

The *world* he had just returned from.

He calmed himself down. He peered through the two-way mirror.

Through the glass.

Into the other room.

He eyed the creature.

The Stranger . . . the *Slug*.

Mitts was far from an expert on Strangers, but he could see, from the way it lay, how its fangs were still—its entire body *still*—that it was dead.

He turned on Doctor Smith. "What happened?" he said. "What's gone *wrong*?"

Doctor Smith smiled gently, working at his touchscreen. "Nothing's *wrong*, Mr Thornestone. You've just returned from a dream. A *dream* of the Stranger's making."

"No," Mitts said, shaking his head. "It wasn't a dream . . . there's *no way* it was a dream."

Doctor Smith held still.

To begin with, he thought he hadn't heard him.

Then, with a wide smile, Doctor Smith finally replied.

"I was hoping you would say that."

———

Later in the day, back in his room, Mitts peered out the window.

He looked down to the garden.

He wore a fluffy, white dressing gown. It had been given to him a few weeks back.

Perhaps to put him at greater comfort.

He could still smell the heavy scent of disinfectant.

It seeped out of his pores.

More than anything, he wished the stench might be replaced by the scent of sulphur.

The smell he had experienced in the other world.

Although it had only been a few hours ago, already it felt like another lifetime.

Mitts had never felt so awake in all his life.

He felt every thought churning through his mind.

His brain throbbed.

But there was no pain.

It was a *pleasant* sensation.

At the same time, his body felt exhausted.

As if it weighed him down.

They had had to bring him to his room in a wheelchair.

When he had attempted to stand—even aided by a pair of escorts—he hadn't been able.

There was a *buzz* at the door.

Mitts remained quiet.

And neither did he bother to look.

To see who it was.

It didn't seem worth his energy.

He continued to stare out across the garden below.

He was vaguely aware of the voice behind him.

He didn't turn.

Carla appeared before him.

Her voice babbled at him . . . *through* him.

Static rattled his skull.

Finally, as if someone had turned the tuning dial a little, the signal came clear.

Mitts slipped back into the 'real world' . . . *his* world.

". . . in the end, and . . ."

Mitts opened his mouth.

Let out a slight groan.

His vocalising apparatus wouldn't obey him.

And then, as had happened with his sense of hearing, everything clicked back into place.

Click.

"What happens to the creatures?" he said. "I mean after you've *used* them?"

Seemingly taken aback by Mitts's sudden lucidity, Carla paused a moment before replying. "They're *clones*, Mitts. That's all. We *made* them to serve our purposes. They wouldn't *exist*—"

But before she'd even finished, Mitts shook his head.

He fixed his eyes on the stone seat down in the garden.

The one he'd been sitting on just that morning.

"No," Mitts broke in, his voice exercising patience. "I asked what you *do* with them."

Carla didn't reply right away.

"It's okay," Mitts went on, "you don't need to consult, you can tell me the truth. I'm *man* enough for the truth."

After another brief pause, Carla responded.

Her voice sounded husky now.

"They die."

Mitts nodded to himself.

He had known that, of course. That much had been apparent.

He had only wanted *her* to say it.

Had only wanted *her* to admit it.

"How many do you use up *spying* on me?" Mitts asked.

"'Spying on you'?" Carla replied, clearly a touch bewildered.

The scent of sulphur became almost too strong to stand.

No, it *was* too strong to stand.

Too strong for him—*a mere mortal*—to resist.

He pushed himself up onto his feet, using the arms of his chair.

"Careful," Carla said, her voice a whisper.

Mitts staggered. He found his balance.

His *physical* strength.

"Why? Are you worried your little *experiments* might be ruined?"

Carla's mouth latched open.

But she said nothing at all.

"How many?" Mitts repeated.

Carla, this time, spoke clearly. "About one a day," she said. "For moderate surveillance."

"And *intensive* surveillance?" Mitts put in.

She swallowed hard.

Mitts caught a whiff of her minty scent.

"It depends on the range—where the target is . . . how *deep* we wish to go . . ."

"To spy on my thoughts—Luca's thoughts—in the Village?"

She blinked rapidly.

Slipped a glance to the door.

This only served to enrage him.

He grabbed hold of her lab coat.

Felt the material tight in his fist.

"*How many?!*"

She trembled in his hold.

They would be here for him.

Any second.

But he had to know.

"Seven . . . eight . . . sometimes more."

Carla sobbed.

Mitts cocked his head to one side.

He stared deeply into Carla's eyes.

Was there a soul there?

Trapped . . . somewhere at the back.

In a cage. Hands curled about the bars.

Peering out with a doleful expression.

Mitts loosened his hold.

Carla took a couple of steps back.

He considered his words.

Calmed himself down.

Then said, "What do you want to achieve?"

" 'Achieve'?" Carla replied, as if it was some kind of alien term.

"What's the *goal* of these experiments? What did you want to *gain* from cloning—from *studying*—these creatures? These *Slugs*?" he added, in a mocking tone.

Carla held herself still.

Mitts took a step toward her.

She took one back from him.

The buzzer on the door went.

She flashed a glance over her shoulder.

He locked his eyes onto hers.

In a thick, throaty voice, he said, "Come in."

———

Mitts didn't need to look. He knew who it was.

Samantha.

Of course . . . who *else* would they send?

They needed to calm him down.

Otherwise everything would be ruined.

Feeling Samantha's gaze lingering over him, Mitts looked to Carla. "I wonder," he said, reaching out for her. "I wonder what might happen if I snap your *neck*."

Carla's eyes widened.

She stared at his hands.

Closing on her.

Coming to *squeeze* her throat.

Mitts stared hard into Carla's eyes.

Her lips quivered.

He thought he could smell blood.

Thick on her breath.

No more of the cool, refreshing, mintiness.

Carla backed into the wall.

Mitts closed the gap.

His fingernails brushed her neck.

His hands found their way about her throat.

He felt her pulse.

The bloody smell drove him on.

He closed his grip.

Squeezed her throat.

Carla trembled.

But she didn't struggle.

Somewhere, at the back of his mind, he heard a gunshot.

He smelled a harsh, intrusive—*mechanical*—odour.

Nothing like sulphur . . . nothing like the sulphur he *craved*.

He waited for the pain.

Looked forward to *embracing* the pain.

He had had enough.

In his head, he counted out the remaining seconds of his life.

They seemed *somehow* important.

He reached a count of ten.

Still no pain.

Carla's body had gone slack.

Surprised, he released her.

She fell to the floor.

Dead.

Blood leaked from her.

Her eyes lolled back in their sockets.

Her mouth latched open.

Mitts turned.

Looked to the door.

Samantha.

Her expression was neutral.

She held a gun.

Tight in her grip.

But it didn't point at him.

It pointed at Carla.

It was as if someone had knocked all the air out of him.

And he was dimly aware of falling to the floor.

———

"Mr Thornestone? Mr Thornestone?"

Mitts was lying down.

He crooked open an eye.

Back on the examination table.

He took in Doctor Smith's wrinkled, leathery features.

This was what he'd wanted.

What he'd wanted all along.

He'd only wanted to go back.

To go back *home*.

Doctor Smith was grave-faced.

He worked at Mitts's scalp. Putting suckers into place. Fiddling with wires.

Arranging *everything*.

When Doctor Smith spoke, it sounded as if his voice was weighed down by a sigh. "A shame," he said. "A *real* shame."

Mitts wasn't aware if Doctor Smith was speaking to himself.

Or if he was speaking for his unseen assistant's benefit.

As before, Mitts felt like an audience member.

A *passenger*.

Present only in body.

Absent in mind.

"We were really counting on you."

" 'Counting on me'?" Mitts repeated.

"Yes. I suppose we'll have to start again. Think of another solution."

". . . Why?"

" 'Why' *indeed*," Doctor Smith replied. "It does seem that we had a good shake, doesn't it?" He shook his head. "But we keep on going—the human *race* keeps going—more resilient than cockroaches." He paused a long while, making some adjustment which Mitts couldn't see. "It's going to take a long time for us to find another like you—another working on the same psychoactive plane as the Slugs . . . if we find one at all."

Mitts felt his mind blurring in and out.

He could smell sulphur now.

Could see dark-purple hills.

Almost there . . . almost there . . . almost *home*.

He glared out over the side of the examination table.

To the other room.

The light was switched off.

The two-way mirror active.

Mitts couldn't see the room on the other side.

But he could *feel* the Stranger there.

He could *feel* its presence.

His family.

His future.

Another future.

Mitts tilted his head back to Doctor Smith.

Again, it felt as if his lips only traced the words.

". . . Luca . . . *why* Luca?"

"Pardon me," Doctor Smith said, leaning over Mitts.

His eyebrows arched up high into his non-existent hairline.

"Oh, was that 'Luca'? Yes, I suppose we could've used her. We could've extracted her. But, truth be told, we were expecting marvellous things from you both. We thought you might be the answer, quite frankly." His lips widened into a smile. "Now, if that doesn't sound desperate, then I really don't know what *does*."

He made his final adjustments to the wires around Mitts's head.

Then gave a slight chuckle.

"I'm sure I sound like an old nut to you. An old man. Death's been tapping me on the shoulder for years." He leaned back, sighed. "The future of the human race will soon be out of my hands."

He nodded to the two-way mirror, to the unseen Stranger on the other side.

"Whatever you're looking for, I hope you find it. In that other world."

Mitts stared back into Doctor Smith's eyes.

He didn't know what to say.

He just wanted to be back . . . back in the *other* world . . . in the *new* world.

His world.

When Doctor Smith spoke again, his voice was a low drawl.

It seemed that he was mumbling to himself.

"Like two strangers in the night," he said.

Mitts strained to trace words with his ears.

He could no longer tell his lips to move.

But it didn't matter.

Not anymore.

"He gone?"

Mitts vaguely heard the assistant's voice in the background.

"Almost," Doctor Smith replied. "Better that we get on with the process before we lose him completely. Don't want him to get rooted down here on this rotten old apple core."

Mitts dimly heard the humming of computer hard drives.

The gentle ebb and flow of his thoughts.

They sloshed.

In and out. In and out.

Like the tide.

At first the scent of sulphur was distant.

Then it was up close.

Before he could really believe it, he was there.

Somewhere else.

Away.

Among the Strangers.

THE END

AUTHOR'S NOTE

Thank you for taking the time to read one of my books. If you would like to hear about my latest releases you can sign up for my newsletter here: www.raymondsflex.com

Thanks for reading!

Raymond S Flex

Strangers In The Night
A Novel